The Killing Hour

by Michael Saxon

Grosvenor House
Publishing Limited

All rights reserved
Copyright **Michael Saxon 2006**

Michael Saxon is hereby identified as author of this
work in accordance with Section 77 of the Copyright, Designs
and Patents Act 1988

This book is published by
Grosvenor House Publishing Ltd
28 – 30 High Street, Guildford, Surrey, GU1 3HY.
www.grosvenorhousepublishing.co.uk

*This book is sold subject to the condition that it shall not, by way of
trade or otherwise, be lent, resold, hired out or otherwise circulated
without the author's or publisher's prior consent in any form of
binding or cover other than that in which it is published and without a similar condition including this condition being imposed on
the subsequent purchaser.*

A CIP record for this book
Is available from the British Library

ISBN 978-1-905529-27-8

The book cover picture is
Copyright to Michael Saxon 2006

Dedication

To the one who got away

Chapter One

His eyes clicked wide open and for a moment he lay motionless. The macabre images were still flashing through his tormented mind; sweat was running from his pores, his body was rigid with fear. Slowly he felt the tension draining away as he started to relax. He tentatively reached out to his left side and felt the comforting warmth of his sleeping wife, lying next to him as she had been every night for the five years since their wedding day.

She didn't know about his dreams. He was always surprised he never woke her from her sleep as he tossed and turned half the night tormented by his visions. Then he had found a bottle of tablets, clearly marked as a sleeping aid, at the back of the medicine cabinet in the bathroom. That, he supposed, explained why she always slept so soundly, waking at seven o'clock every morning like clockwork. It never crossed his mind to ask her why she needed tablets for sleeping. If she wanted him to know then she would tell him; he suspected it was the stress of work and could empathise with that. He returned her bottle to where it was and thought no more of it.

He swung his legs over the side of the bed and made his way to the en suite, where he languished under the red hot shower for maybe ten minutes. He soon felt sufficiently cleansed to dress and make breakfast before leaving for work, which was an hour's drive at this time of day. He kissed his still sleeping wife and looked lovingly at her as her lips formed into a half smile. It would be half an hour before she woke to start her daily routine, by which time he would be about half way to the office. He collected his jacket from the banister and closed the door quietly behind him before turning to walk the few feet to his vehicle, ready now for the day ahead with a clear mind and a refreshed body.

James Elliot considered himself to be an average sort of chap. He was good looking to the point of being a 'pretty boy'; his features and build, he admitted, were not very masculine. He was slight in stature, being wiry rather than muscular, and wore his hair slightly longer than perhaps he should; but he was popular with his colleagues at work and that pleased him. He wondered how they would see him if they knew the torment he was suffering behind those deep blue eyes and dazzling white smile.

As he drove to work his mind played again the dreams he had been having that night, always fragmented, but so vivid, and seemingly becoming more frequent. They had started just after his wedding day, something he remembered because they were so disturbing, and over the last five years had increased from one every few months, to being weekly, and now, it seemed, almost every night.

He shook his head and tried to concentrate on his driving, but he kept drifting back to the grisly images he was seeing in his sleeping hours. Although they were interspersed with other unconnected images, the horrific sight of the headless torsos kept recurring. The heads, still dripping with blood, clearly hacked from the bodies in a most savage way, were sat on a shelf, eyes wide and staring in looks of sheer terror, lined up in some sort of gruesome display.

His head snapped up, clearing instantly at the sound of a car horn blasting at him. He had been veering across the central lines in the road and had almost collided with an oncoming vehicle.

He really had to do something about this, he thought; maybe he could talk to Davies in the Behavioural Section. He was a well regarded psychiatrist and maybe a chat with him could help with the problem. He determined to make an appointment that morning as he drove up to the gatehouse of the Clinical Research Centre where he worked as a pharmacist, and stopped at the barrier.

The security officer came out of his office with clipboard in hand to sign him in and check his security pass as he had done nearly every day for three years. It was a routine which slightly irritated Elliot because it was so repetitive. He thanked God he had a good career; he was sure he would go mad doing that sort of work.

'Good morning Mr Elliot, how are you today?' was the robotic greeting from the man in the uniform.

'Good morning, Barton,' came the automatic reply from his own lips as he passed through the open barrier and drove to his parking space ready to begin his working day.

thinking, new leadership, a different perspective on things were needed, and she knew she was the one who could deliver all of these things. She had already made some progress, spending hours each night going over all the files, trying to find some clue, some small piece of information that could lead her to the killer; maybe something innocuous, seemingly insignificant until tied in with other information. She knew there must be something in those files and she was determined that she would unearth whatever was in them and use it to bring this sick individual to justice, something which a number of her colleagues had failed to do so far. Each had paid the price, being moved sideways to other jobs but knowing their careers would go no further. She was determined that would not happen to her; the combination of rising through the ranks and her university degree in Sociology would give her the edge needed to see this case through to a successful conclusion.

The meeting had been called at short notice after another murder victim had been found by a team of refuse collectors in the early hours of the morning. They had stumbled across the body as they emptied bins around the back streets of the city centre. None of them had ever seen a dead person before, and now they were confronted by the sight, not just of a body, but one which had been decapitated and mutilated. It was no surprise to the first detectives on the scene to find two of the team vomiting and all of them in a state of deep shock.

The street had been taped off by uniform. The police photographer was in the process of recording the scene from every possible angle for later examination. Nearby a group of forensic scientists were waiting for him to finish before they could start their painstaking search of the area and carry out a thorough examination of what was once a human being, but now resembled something you might see hanging in an abattoir.

Andrea Collins had been the first of the task force to arrive at the crime scene and, after a quick visual examination of the victim, she had decided it was indeed another link in their chain of killings and so had called a meeting for later that morning with all the members of her team.

The injuries were almost identical to the last victim. There were massive wounds to the neck where the head had been sawn from the torso in what must have been a frenzied attack. It had been established that the victims had all been alive at the time of decapitation and that was horrific enough. But the thing that disturbed Collins most was the other injuries. Each of the victims had been stabbed in the chest, destroying vital organs, and every one had then had the heart cut from them. Not in a clinical way, but in a savage, hacking, and tearing manner, which had left the bodies looking like pieces of butchered meat.

Fighting back the nausea she had made a quick search of the immediate area, but, as in every other case, the head and the heart were nowhere to be seen. This both worried and puzzled her; where were they, and why had they been removed and taken away? If they had been dumped somewhere else one would have turned up by now, but there had been no reported cases of heads found anywhere in the country. As ridiculous as that sounded there had been an alert put out to all forces, discreetly, to keep an eye open for bodiless heads.

That thought almost made her laugh but she kept her composure, thinking that nerves must be getting the better of her. Maybe someone was collecting them, she mused. It had happened in other cases she'd read about, mainly in the United States. She remembered reading a paper about killers keeping trophies from their crimes. Just like some people would collect ornamental items or memorabilia, these serial killers would keep pieces of clothing, or even body parts from their crimes for some reason no-one would ever understand. How could anyone ever come close to understanding such a twisted mind, she wondered, and as that thought passed through her mind something clicked in her head. She remembered a research paper she'd read a few months previously, written by an eminent psychiatrist. It was about psychological profiling, something relatively new to this country but which had apparently been used for a number of years in the United States with some notable successes, as had been the use of psychics to lead the police to certain places where they would find vital evidence, or even the location where a crime had been committed.

Like most people she was dubious of such practises, thinking them to be nothing more than mumbo jumbo, but now she was prepared to set that thought aside. At this point in the investigation, she reasoned, surely it was worth exploring every avenue open to her, even one that went against what she considered logic. So she made a note to track down the author of that particular research document and make an appointment with him as soon as possible.

The meeting was tense; another murder, and still no clues to work with. Collins wasn't happy and she let her colleagues know, in no uncertain terms, that she expected, no, demanded better performances from the team. She wanted results before the story became public knowledge. That was something she would have preferred but the word had come from on high, as sometimes happened in particularly bad cases, that this was to be kept under wraps. It wasn't in the public interest for the public to know that a mass murderer was on the loose and now killing people at the rate of one a week. Politicians were such idiots she thought angrily; not in the government's interest was more like the truth, but she had to follow orders, even if she knew the media could be used to help their efforts. Well, there was an election coming up, and one thing politicians were always good at was getting things prioritised, the main priority always being self preservation.

After her team had all left the room to perform their assigned duties, she wandered over to the far wall, where all the victims were listed and stood quietly looking at the photographs. If only they could talk, she thought, just one word might be all that was needed to solve this whole messy affair. She walked to the door, exited, and locked it behind her, taking with her the discs she had downloaded from the computer. She would take them home and spend what was left of the day poring over every scrap of information that they contained, in the hope that she would spot something she may have missed earlier on.

Chapter Three

At the Clinical Research Centre in the north Cheshire countryside, James Elliot was having a consultation with his colleague Dr. Davies. Elliot had explained about the terrifying nature of his dreams and the effect they were having on his sleep pattern, in the hope that Davies could offer some explanation and perhaps suggest a way to help him overcome the problem. Davies had listened patiently, taking notes and then walking him back through each moment, asking questions and taking more notes. It was becoming rather uncomfortable for Elliot now as he listened to his own voice, in a detached sort of way, explaining in detail the gruesome sights he was seeing.

The heads were all sat on some sort of shelving in a dimly lit room, strands of sinew and skin trailing from the neck wounds. They all had wide staring eyes, and all of them seemed to be looking directly at him. He was sweating now, as though he was back in his dreams, his mouth dry, and fear gripping him as he started to tremble. At that point, Davies, seeing the effect his probing was having on him, decided to end the interview. 'James,' he said, 'I think that's enough for one session, but I would like to see you again. I think together we can get to the bottom of this and help you get back to normal. Take the rest of the day off, go home and relax, and make an appointment with my secretary on your way out for the end of the week.'

Elliot made his exit and hurried out into the fresh air; he would take the doctor's advice and put his feet up for the rest of the day. He arrived home to find a note from Amy, his wife, on the kitchen table:

'Going shopping after work, will be home about seven. Amy, x.'

Damn, he thought, it would be nice to see her awake once in a while. It seemed they were always just missing each other, always too tired to spend time together. He couldn't remember the last time they had shared a drink, had a meal and a good chat. He should speak to her and make more of an effort, he thought, as he sank into his favourite armchair and closed his eyes.

Amy heard him come in but decided to leave by the back door. She knew he would want to talk and really there was nothing left to say. The marriage had crumbled from their wedding night and she wondered why she had stayed for so long with someone she no longer loved. Perhaps it was the security and peace of mind, not having to worry about where the next meal was coming from. That was something she had experienced too much of in her earlier years, living with an alcoholic mother who spent most of their income feeding her habit, until, in the end, she had followed her husband, Amy's father, to an early grave.

There had been one consolation for Amy and that was the property her father had invested in many years before for a price of a few hundred pounds. He had known he would die early and had wisely changed the deeds so that Amy was the sole owner. He had made her promise not to tell her mother about the house; he could see even then the way his wife would go to any lengths to procure her supply of alcohol, and he was not going to let her sell the property and drink away his only daughter's inheritance. On his deathbed he had given Amy one last piece of advice, and that was to keep her house no matter what the future held for her. It would always be her little bit of security for a rainy day, a place to retreat to if ever she needed somewhere to get away from things for a while, and it had proved to be very sound advice. She had met James soon after her mother's death and within twelve months had given notice to her landlord, moved in with James and, shortly afterwards, following a brief engagement they had married.

They argued on their wedding day. Amy was suspicious that James had slept with one of the bridesmaids the night before. Why else would she see him leaving her friend's house early in the morning, looking dishevelled, when he was supposedly out having a stag night drink with a few of his friends? She didn't want to believe it but when she had confronted him, regrettably almost immediately after the wedding ceremony, he had as good as admitted his guilt. That had led to a tearful and acrimonious end to some good friendships, and what should have been the happiest day of her life. Later on they had argued more and James had struck out, leaving her with a cut lip and a badly bruised cheek. At that moment she had vowed to have revenge on him. She felt she had been duped; the person before her was not the James she had come to love but the real James, violent, untrustworthy, and manipulative. At least he didn't know about her inheritance, at least she had somewhere to go if she needed to. She had silently thanked her father for his foresight as she looked up at James's smirking face, a feeling of pure hatred raging through her head as he stood over her, mocking her, inviting her to hit him back. I will have my day, she thought; she wasn't going to play his game. It would be her who chose the time and place to take her revenge.

Almost every day since then she had been to the old farmhouse. It was set in eight acres of meadow and woodland, a secluded hideaway with its own long driveway up from the nearest road, which itself was little more than a track but suited her perfectly. She didn't want any unwelcome visitors or any nosey neighbours calling every five minutes. She had grown to love the place and had spent hours decorating and scrubbing from top to bottom until it was just as she wanted it. She was sure that James didn't know about this place. Once she had left a letter from her solicitor on the kitchen table and was terrified that he might have read it, but he had never mentioned anything about it so she had convinced herself that her secret must be safe.

Her very special place was the barn. It was a large rectangular building, made from random stone blocks up to the chamber floor and a timber-clad frame sat atop the stonework, with a window at each gable end. On the ground floor, though, she had discovered a trapdoor, and found to her delight that it led to a cellar-type room underneath the barn floor which was dimly lit by a single pendant light fitting. She had spent hours down there, cleaning and dusting until everything was spotless, and had even painted the shelves that covered each wall. This would be ideal for her collection, she had thought; there was ample room here, and even though it would take her years to fill all the shelves she had all the time in the world.

Amy wandered over to the far wall of the cellar where she kept the centre piece of her collection. A large decorative urn was sat in the middle of the shelf. On the front were painted two eyes, wide and staring, looking directly at her; inside were mothers' ashes. A pity, she thought, that mother had been cremated, or she could have kept her head as the centre piece; still, the eyes were very lifelike and she knew mother could see her through them, watching every step she took on her road to redemption. Each time she bought a new head back for the collection it was placed in front of her mother's urn for her approval, and, as mother studied each new piece, Amy would take the heart she had collected and slowly chew her way through it until she had devoured every last piece.

She knew that one day soon mother would give her approval and tell Amy that she loved her, which was all she wanted. All those endless hours of being told she was worthless and ugly, that no one loved her or would ever look at her, would end, she knew, because everybody in this room was always looking at her. They followed her every movement with their wide, staring eyes as she performed whatever task she was doing, and soon mother would have to recognise her achievement. She was no longer the heartless person her mother had insisted she was; all the hearts she had taken and eaten had built and strengthened her own heart. At last she felt that she was a warm, caring, and loving individual and all she needed now to complete her happiness was mother's blessing.

Amy removed the fresh heart she had taken the night before from the waterproof bag on the table, and with her other hand lifted the head by the hair, holding it up, studying the features. Such a pretty face, she thought; with lovely dark brown almost black hair, sparkling white teeth and ice blue eyes. It would be a nice addition to her collection.

With the head held up for mother to study, Amy sank her teeth into the bloodied organ in her hand, taking a large bite, tearing at the piece with her teeth until it ripped away and she could chew it as she watched mothers reaction to her latest offering. As she devoured the heart, blood trickling down her chin, she could see the scorn in the eyes, mother still wasn't happy Amy could tell. Well she would keep on collecting and feeding her heart until the day mother smiled and said,' Amy I love you' it was so simple, just four words and her life would be complete. Amy would never understand why mother was so cruel to her, maybe one day she would explain, but for now all she could do was continue her quest.

It was dark when James woke up, still in his armchair. He felt so tired these days; the lack of sleep was catching up with him. He rose from his chair and went upstairs on weary legs; all he wanted to do was get into bed and sleep a dreamless sleep. Amy must have arrived home while he slept. She was in bed, dead to the world for all intents. She looked so peaceful lying there as he leaned over to kiss her lips and whisper goodnight in her ear. James undressed and crawled in besides her, lying on his back, and within seconds was fast asleep.

But sleep was not easy for James that night, and as he entered the dream phase of the sleep pattern he found himself once again in the room with the shelves. Looking slowly around the room he could see the lifeless heads, dozens of them, looks of terror frozen forever on their faces. The eyes that stared so that they all seemed to be looking directly at him, accusing him; why was he here, he thought, why were they looking at him?

His gaze settled on the far side of the room where a single wooden table stood, about three feet away from the wall, right at the centre of the shelves. He felt himself drawn towards it, a morbid fascination overcoming his sheer terror. His feet moved slowly, mechanically, taking him nearer. His heart was pounding in his chest, his head felt light; he could hear the blood rushing through his veins as he approached the table. His eyes were locked on the bag; it sat there, gaping open, inviting him to look inside. As he reached the table he heard the whisper, 'Amy'.

His head jerked up to where the voice had come from and he looked into a pair of eyes that seemed to bore into his very soul. They were painted on a vase or some sort of urn, but he felt they were alive and were staring at him with a look of pure malevolence blazing from them. He was rooted to the spot, unable to move; he wanted to turn and run from this place, he wanted to scream, but nothing came out. Instead he saw his hand moving towards the bag as if it was someone else's. He reached inside, feeling something wet and sticky, and as his hand emerged from the bag his mind screamed at the sight of a heart gripped in his fingers. He watched as his hand lifted and came towards his face, he felt his mouth open and as the heart touched his lips he at last screamed as he sat bolt upright in bed, shaking with fear and horror, sweat running from him in streams.

His eyes registered that he was in his own bedroom and that it had indeed been just a dream. He felt like he was drowning, a feeling of sheer panic pervading his senses. Why had he heard his wife's name whispered? What had these dreams got to do with Amy? He rose from the bed as quietly as he could so as not to wake her and went to the bathroom where he turned on the cold water faucet. He put his head under the cool refreshing flow until his mind had cleared and the panic slowly began to subside.

Chapter Four

Andrea Collins was concerned. She had received a call from a journalist who worked for one of the national tabloids, one with a reputation as an excellent investigative reporter. When she had answered the call with 'Collins, task force, hello?' she knew she had slipped up. The caller identified herself as Kate Mitchell and asked for confirmation of a string of murders she had heard about from a 'source'. Damn, thought Collins, who the hell had talked? How much had they leaked? It had to be one of her colleagues who had been removed from the task force and now felt they had an axe to grind.

It would be better to find out how much Mitchell knew and try to come to some sort of agreement with the journalist, perhaps appeal to her sense of public duty. But that, she knew, would never work with a hard nosed professional like Mitchell. Her only sense of duty would be to get her name on the yearly awards list for unearthing a major exclusive. The story was massive; probably the biggest manhunt ever undertaken in the country, and it had been kept quiet for political reasons, which made it even more explosive. It wasn't fair, thought Collins, having her hands tied for political expediency. She had pleaded to bring the media in, she had insisted that they could help with the case, but she had been overruled. Now it had leaked and it would be her who took all the flak. 'Politicians don't interfere with criminal investigations' would be the line from the Home Office. She would be the sacrificial lamb if things went badly wrong. She knew with certainty that her career would come to a grinding halt if she handled this badly.

She cursed Mitchell again for her ruthless ambition. Her career came before any other interest, and it infuriated Collins when people were like that, no matter how much damage it caused to others. Still, she had no choice but to work with the journalist, and so she had taken down Mitchell's number and promised to call her later that day to arrange a meeting, strictly off the record.

They met the next day at a small bistro just off Deansgate in the city centre, both ordering coffee before making their way to a quiet table in the corner of the bar, away from the bustle of the lunchtime trade. Taking seats opposite each other they spent several minutes in silence, studying one another. Each liked what they saw, seeing before them an attractive, confident woman, and recognising in each other the determination and resolve that made them high flyers in their respective fields.

Collins was first to speak.

'Alright, Kate. Tell me what you know, and we will see how we can help each other.'

Mitchell had nothing to lose. She had received a single short call informing her that there was an investigation underway involving a serial killer with several deaths to their credit. She also knew that a media blackout had been imposed, because the authorities feared public unrest over the number of deaths and the length of time the killer had been on the loose.

Mitchell hated authority with a vengeance; people in positions of authority always fell into the same trap of cover ups and deceit, wrongly thinking that they were protecting the public. In reality, she knew the public would prefer some honesty from their leaders, and just for once to hear a political figure say 'we made mistakes, we are sorry but we are working on putting them right.' Instead they were fed denials and lies, half-truths and distortions while the problems they knew existed went unsolved because the powers that be were so obsessed with perception and image. Substance had become unimportant, but not to Mitchell. She had made it her life's work to uncover corruption and incompetence in public life and she could smell a big story here, one that could rock the establishment, and she intended to do whatever was necessary to obtain that story.

Mitchell outlined what little she knew, making a couple of guesses to give the impression she knew a little more than she did, but Collins was experienced too and could also read between the lines. She was satisfied that Kate didn't really know that much and that put Collins in the driving seat which was just where she liked to be. Kate Mitchell needed her more than she needed Kate Mitchell.

'So what can you tell me Andrea?' was Mitchell's direct question.

'None of what I tell you can go to print, Kate; I need your word on that. If you cooperate I will give you the full story, but you mustn't print it until the killer is safely locked behind bars. No names, just a source, because that would cost me my career. Even if I solve the case our masters are very vindictive with people who don't follow their rules.'

She had taken the plunge now and would have to trust Kate. That wasn't something she did easily, but if she was going to solve this case she was going to have to take a few risks. She decided to be generous, and launched into a detailed explanation of the events of the last five years. The look of incredulity on Kate's face was a picture to behold; how often, she wondered, could you shock a seasoned journalist like Kate Mitchell into open mouthed silence? Collins savoured the moment, it was probably a first and last. It would be followed by outrage and indignation at the cover up, and the breathtaking incompetence of the system. Kate Mitchell would get her teeth into this and, like a terrier, hold on doggedly until she had exposed the whole stinking mess. Collins relaxed a little, barely suppressing a smile; Mitchell was easy to provoke and predict. As she grasped the enormity of the situation her cheeks coloured, her mouth opening to let out a string of profanities that would have made a dock worker blush. Collins seized the moment and made her pitch.

'Now Kate, there's nothing we can do for those girls. All we can do is see this bastard brought to justice. That's where you come in. I want you to run with this story, and I'm going to pass you information, sensitive details about the case. Hopefully we can provoke a response, put a bit of pressure on him. Make out we have more leads than we do, maybe suggest an arrest is imminent. If we can make him feel like the net is closing in, panic him a little, that's when these people get sloppy, and that's when they make mistakes.'

'And you nail the bastard,' Mitchell growled. Excellent, Collins thought to herself. She's onboard.

In the last few days she had studied papers concerning these types of cases and in many of them the serial killers were apparently playing some sort of game. They would see themselves as superior to every one else, even going to the extent of giving clues and in some cases making contact and mocking the police teams that were pursuing them. But somewhere along the line they would trip up; thinking themselves overclever was often their downfall and this was what Collins wanted to discuss with Dr. Davies, the author of one of one of the papers she had read, at the meeting she had arranged with him for the following morning.

The two women shook hands on their deal and agreed to speak each evening about any developments in the case. They both saw the need to keep their arrangement under wraps and had decided to contact each other by phone only, except in circumstances where they might need to pass over written or photographic material. Collins stood and left the bar, followed a few minutes later by Mitchell whose head was still spinning from the revelations she had heard in the last hour.

Chapter Five

The next morning, Collins drove from the city centre out into the Cheshire countryside for her meeting with Dr. Davies. He was the eminent psychiatrist whom, she had learned, was the author of a number of papers on psychological profiling in recent years. He had actually already worked with a number of police forces both here and in the United States, gaining himself a growing reputation as one of the leading experts in the field.

She arrived at the research centre in the heart of the countryside and as she walked to the building took in the fresh air and excellent views. It would be nice working out here in these surroundings, she thought, away from the bustle and dirt of the big city. She had lived in a place like this as a child and the love of open space had always remained with her. She set those thoughts aside as she was led into a plush reception room by a pleasant young man who looked as though he had not slept much the night before. She smiled and thanked him as he left the room. James was wondering what a Detective Chief Inspector was doing here as he carried on to the next floor where his laboratory was situated.

Collins remembered she had been that age once, living life to the full, staying up all night to party or with a lover. Now she still stayed up all hours but her life was all work and that was something she had to change. After this case was solved, she vowed, she would take a holiday and try to get some sort of social life. A secretary appeared, breaking into her daydreams.

'Dr. Davies is ready to receive you now.'

Davies greeted her and settled into an easy chair opposite Collins. He waited until his secretary had served them coffee and left the room before speaking.

'Well, Detective Collins, from what I hear you have a serial killer on your hands. I assume you would like my opinion on the case?'

'Yes, Doctor, that's exactly why I'm here. Your reputation in the field tells me you are the best.'

Davies smiled. Professional pride, thought Collins; from reporters to serial killers to psychiatrists. She knew how to work people; but she was forgetting that he was also a psychiatrist, and he knew how to work people as well.

'If you give me a rundown of the case so far, I'll do my best to help in any way I can,' he said.

Collins gave him a brief outline of the case. She told him of the way that the girls were murdered, the dates, and the locations. She didn't give him the files; she was reluctant to give anyone outside her team access to the complete case. If he needed further information she could deliver it another time. Davies listened patiently while she explained the details to him. When she was finished he leant back in his chair, fingers interlocking, and gave Collins a look that made her think he was analysing her.

'Without looking at the files, Detective, I can't really form a full profile. However, judging by what you have told me this case would seem to fit into a classic pattern. I have come across several similar cases before.'

Collins nodded. 'Can you at least give me some idea of what sort of person we should be looking for?' asked Collins.

'You will be looking for a single white male, 20 to 30 years old; someone who suffered abuse as a child, and might have records at social services from a spell in care. He has a pathological hatred for women. He may be a loner and possibly a drifter, or maybe someone who travels for their work.'

'That's very broad, Doctor. How would we recognise him?'

'You wouldn't recognise him. He will appear quite normal; he may even have a good job and a nice house. He has probably lived a respectable life up until he started killing. It can be like a switch being thrown in the mind; one day normal, the next, a mass killer. They are compelled to kill. They can be unpredictable, to a certain degree, but generally speaking these types are usually caught when they make a mistake. Of course, sometimes they kill themselves when they have completed whatever they set out to do.'

Collins stayed another half hour, asking questions and making notes. Davies' detached, clinical attitude to the slaughter of so many girls may have been off-putting, but she knew it was the only way to deal with these things; nobody involved could afford to get emotional. She couldn't begin to understand the twisted world of these people, and Davies would be a valuable addition to her team. Both of them were pushed for time so they kept it as brief as possible. Collins agreed to send more information to Davies so he could do a more detailed profile for her. They shook hands at the reception area and Collins headed back towards the city, armed with a new insight into the mind of a serial killers. It was a daunting task that lay before her but she was confident that she was up to it. She had a good team and good technology; between them, she was sure they would crack the case.

Chapter Six

Amy was awake and ready for an evening's work. She was in her favourite black dress, the one she always wore when she went out to meet her new collection pieces. They always fell for her in that; she knew she looked good, with her slim body and striking features crowned with long, wavy black hair. She made sure her hair was perfectly groomed and stood before the mirror admiring her self. She liked what she saw; she may have been twenty-six but she didn't look a day over twenty-one.

Her mood changed and her cheeks flushed as she thought of mother's mocking words. Why couldn't mother see that she had become a beautiful and worthy person? She would show mother one day, she thought angrily as she quietly closed the front door behind herself, and she would show James as well. She had left him when he had drifted into a deep sleep and now she was in her world, one where people noticed and admired her.

She got in to her car, a two-year old, five-door Ford with plenty of boot space, and drove towards Sheffield city centre. She hadn't collected in Sheffield yet, and it would be a nice change to be in new surroundings.

Amy had tried a couple of clubs and was now in a third which seemed much busier and had better music to dance to.

She loved to dance and knew that when she did people would notice her and very soon she would have them moving in on her, asking to dance with her.

The men were persistent and a nuisance, but that couldn't be avoided; she gave them short shrift and they soon scuttled away with red faces, tails between their legs. She loved to see their faces when she belittled them, what fragile egos they had she thought with a self satisfied smile playing across her face as she gyrated her hips in the most provocative manner she could manage.

She was drawing admiring glances from some of the girls in the room now and soon picked out a gorgeous looking blonde of about twenty-one with a figure to die for. Mother will love this one she thought, as she lowered her eyelids and parted her lips slightly, her seductive look she liked to call it, and sure enough the blonde was making eye contact with her now.

She continued to dance slowly and seductively, tilting her head slightly in invitation to the blonde who was now gliding across the dance floor towards her, a smile coming to her face as she reached Amy.

'Hi, my name's Sam,' she purred with a look that would melt the hardest of hearts. 'Hi, my name's Jayne,' said Amy in her own sultry voice. She could tell by the girl's eyes that she would be sitting on her shelf before the break of day.

Sam was slightly drunk, and Amy could tell she wanted her. Her sexuality wasn't an issue; her only concern was that no one saw them leave together. If Sam did tell any of her friends she was leaving, it would be with a girl called Jayne. Amy didn't want to jeopardise her chance to finish her collection.

They danced for a while together, making small talk; Amy could be very charming and knew how to seduce someone. She asked Sam if she would like to join her for drinks at the hotel where she was staying while she was in town on business. Sam was impressed, she could tell, even more so when Amy told her that she was a collector of rare fine art pieces and that even though only a few people had ever seen her collection, Sam was welcome to view it if she would like to. It was nice to find someone who was interested, she told Sam. Amy watched as Sam went over to the table where her two friends sat and said her goodbyes for the evening.

Her excitement was beginning to stir as she waited for Sam to collect her hand bag and coat before joining her at the door, where she hugged her warmly before they left the club, hand in hand like the young lovers Sam thought they were going to be. Amy's sense of anticipation was growing by the minute; she had to take a deep breath and remain calm, careful not to let her excitement overtake her emotions.

She led Sam to her car where, after a passionate kiss, she produced a small flask containing an alcoholic fruit drink which was very popular these days. Sam took a drink and Amy told her to finish it.

'I can't have any if I'm driving,' she explained. Within five minutes of taking her first sip Sam was drifting into unconsciousness. The drug Amy used never failed; it would last about half an hour, by which time she would have Sam safely tied up and ready for the ritual.

She drove to the deserted industrial unit that she had spotted earlier on. She pulled up, checking for onlookers; the street was silent as the grave. Certain that the coast was clear she walked around to the passenger door of her car, opened it, and dragged the now unconscious Sam from her seat.

Even though she was a dead weight, Amy easily picked her up and leaned forward so that her limp body slid over her own shoulder. Amy straightened up and opened the car boot, reaching in to pick up the holdall in which she kept her accessories; she walked away from the car to the side of the warehouse and kicked open the rotten door.

The noise echoed around the building but Amy knew no one would be around at this hour, so she continued into the large empty space before her until she found a metal pillar that was ideal for her purpose.

She held Sam up against the pillar while she secured the nylon rope to each hand, then passed the rope through the metal work and pulled so that Sam had her hands above her head and to either side, in a sort of crucifixion pose. Amy reached back into her bag and produced a pair of scissors, with which she cut through the upper clothing Sam was wearing to leave her naked from the waist upwards. She cut a strip of the cloth from the skimpy top and tied it around Sam's mouth to act as a gag. Of course, Amy would have preferred to hear Sam talk to her, to ask why she was doing this, to plead and beg for her release, just like all the others; but it would be too noisy when she screamed, and the less attention she drew to herself the better.

She stood back and looked at her watch. Less than five minutes and Sam would wake. The excitement was building within Amy now, her whole body tingling with anticipation at the look she knew would be on the girl's face, first bewilderment, then horror as she realised she was at Amy's mercy. Not knowing what was going to happen would bring the fear; Amy had seen it so many times before but still never lost the thrill as she studied the faces before her going through a whole range of emotions.

Sam began to stir, her eyes slowly opening and trying to focus in the dim light coming through the open door way and broken windows from the street light outside. She could see Amy standing before her, smiling; she looked up to see her hands bound to the pillar and began to struggle. Panic was creeping into her face as she began to sob, the sound muffled by the gag around her mouth. Sam was trying to talk but growing more agitated because the only way out of this situation was to try and reason with Amy and she was unable to do that while she was restricted by the cloth that was cutting into the corners of her mouth.

Amy watched silently as Sam strained against her bonds, the fear on her face showing clearly now. Amy's excitement was getting more intense; she could feel herself trembling and knew it was time to release Sam from her torment. Amy reached down and removed her tools from the holdall at her side, slowly walking the few paces to where Sam still struggled to release herself, her eyes fixated on Amy's hands. In one she held a meat cleaver and in the other what looked like some kind of hunting knife, with a serrated back edge to the blade. Her eyes lifted to Amy's face in a desperate, silent plea for mercy; she looked into wide, staring eyes and saw that manic smile. She knew at that moment that Amy was totally mad, and with the strength of a trapped animal she tried franticly to break free. Her bonds were too well secured and now that Amy was only inches from her face she could feel Amy's breath on her cheek. It was too much for Sam; she felt her bladder open and the urine running down her legs. With her last remaining coherent thought Sam realised Amy was talking to her and strained to hear what she was saying. Her heartbeat and the blood rushing around her head seemed to deafen her, but the words were coming through now.

'Don't worry Sam, I am going to set you free now,' she said in a soothing voice. 'You're going to come home and meet my mother, she will love you.'

Sam was confused as Amy leaned forward and kissed her on the forehead. The manic smile was still fixed on her face, but Amy had clearly said that she was going to release her. Sam felt a glimmer of hope and relaxed slightly; she felt something hot on her body around her ribs, and as the heat grew she looked down to see Amy's hand, wrapped around the knife that she was slowly pushing into her body.

Her mind reeled. The pain was not getting through her fear yet, but she knew it would and she knew she was going to die. Amy slowly pushed the knife in to the hilt, changing its path as she hit a rib, then let go of it, leaving it protruding from Sam's rib cage. There was only a trickle of blood, but that would change to a flow when she pulled the knife out.

Amy reached up and took a handful of Sam s hair, pulling her head back to expose the throat, and brought her other hand up with the cleaver gripped firmly in it. Sam watched in morbid, detached fascination, her eyes wide and fixed, as the cleaver swung through the air towards her throat.

She was beyond emotion now. Her mind had accepted that her death was inevitable and, even as the cleaver cut into her neck, severing her windpipe, she was trying to rationalise what was happening to her. She felt the rush of cool air into her torn windpipe and the blood flowing into her lungs, the excruciating pain in her chest as the next blow severed her spinal cord, and her last thought as her life ended was a simple 'Why?'

Amy was exhilarated, as she always was at the taking of another piece for her collection. She had set Sam free, just like she had told her she would; now, using her hunting knife, she quickly hacked away the last remaining sinews to release the head and dropped it into her holdall. She then began cutting open the chest with rough sawing movements, exposing the heart. She gripped it with one hand and severed the connecting tubes with the knife in her other hand, before dropping it into her holdall alongside the head.

She washed the blood from her hands and face with the bottled water from her holdall and checked her hair was tidy with her compact mirror. She placed her cleaning materials back in her bag before picking it up, and then walked out of the building without a backward glance, focusing now only on getting to the barn to present her latest offering to mother.

James woke with a start; another nightmare had disturbed his sleep, and he rushed again to the bathroom to splash his face with cold water. His head was pounding relentlessly, he was sweating, and his hands trembled as he held them before his eyes. Looking in the mirror he was shocked to see how gaunt his face was becoming; he looked as though he hadn't slept at all that night. What was happening to him? Was he losing his mind? His dreams seemed so real, as though he was actually there in the room, but he knew he was looking through someone else's eyes. That night he had seen a ring on the hand which held the knife as it plunged into the girl's ribcage; it was a slim hand but a strong one, the ring a plain gold band on the wedding finger. He never wore his wedding ring so he knew it was not his own hand, but it was still deeply disturbing that he should be seeing these sorts of images. Tomorrow was the appointment with Davies, and it couldn't come a moment too soon for his liking.

Chapter Seven

Collins had just arrived in Sheffield after receiving a call from the Yorkshire Police Force concerning a murder which bore all the hallmarks of the case she was running. She had taken a Detective Sergeant with her as she didn't like the drive over the Snake Pass, especially when speed was required and she felt much safer with Paul at the wheel. He had received advanced training and handled the vehicle with ease as he negotiated the treacherous bends smoothly and with confidence.

She had made a number of phone calls on the way over to ensure that the forensics and pathology people would all be at the murder scene. She had also left strict orders that nothing should be disturbed until she arrived to take charge, an order which had prompted the usual resentful attitude from her counterpart in the Sheffield service. When would these people realise they were all on the same side? She stirred from her thoughts as the car came to a halt outside a disused, shabby-looking industrial unit on the outskirts of the city.

'I'm Detective Chief Inspector Collins,' she said to the officer who was there to greet her, and was pleasantly surprised to be met by a promise of full cooperation and any assistance he could offer. The verbal lashing she had given to her colleague over the phone must have had the required effect, she thought with a satisfied smile. She thanked him as they entered the building; she noted the door, which looked as if it had been wrenched or kicked off its hinges and was lying on the floor. Beyond that someone had set lights up. The mains supply must have been disconnected; at least someone was using their brains and acting professionally, Collins thought.

She made her way towards the light, where a small group of police officers were gathered. 'Good morning everyone, I'm DCI Collins, head of the Task Force,' she said in introduction. Best to let them know who is in charge from the outset, she thought. A few good mornings were returned as they parted so that Collins could approach the body. She knew they were watching her face to see what sort of reaction she would have and was determined not to show any sign of weakness. Hiding her feelings was something learned over the years in a profession still dominated by a male culture. But when she saw the body her stomach turned and she had to use all of her will power to keep her face impassive, as she studied what was left of this unfortunate human being.

The body was tied by the wrists, arms stretched outwards and upwards towards where the rope was secured around the pillar. It was obviously a young woman; she still wore her high shoes and short skirt but her upper clothing had been removed. There was a gaping chest wound where the heart had been removed and the head was missing from the torso.

Collins couldn't remember seeing such a shocking picture as the one before her in a career which spanned twenty years and had covered many murders. This just seemed more horrific somehow. Maybe it was because they were all girls in their early twenties; it just seemed such a senseless waste of life, all of them killed without apparent motive.

Her mind was wandering, thinking about how the girl's family might react if they ever found out the truth of what had happened here, what sort of hell they were going to go through when they were told their daughter or sister had been murdered. Her head snapped around and she barked a question at one of the detectives.

'Have we identified her yet?'

'Her name is Samantha Harding, boss; aged twenty, single, still living at home with her parents. We have people round there now interviewing them.'

'Good,' she said. 'I want everything you get, collated and forwarded to me as soon as you have it. Check her movements Saturday night; she must have had friends. Maybe one of them saw her talking to someone.' She took a second to compose herself. 'We have to get this bastard before he strikes again. I want doors rattled, I want beds emptied, I want every known pervert and weirdo hauled in, and I want it yesterday. See to it now.'

The pathologist had determined that death had occurred approximately twenty- four hours previously, which made it early Sunday morning. It was a good bet that the girl had been in one of the many night clubs around town. Somebody must have seen her; maybe this time they would get the break they needed.

'Detective, you may want to look at this,' said one of the forensic team.

Collins moved nearer to where three of them were doing a painstaking search of the floor. There was quite a layer of dust on the floor and so footprints had been left near to the body. She looked down, not recognising what she was seeing; there was a small half- round mark and a larger, more pointed one close to it

'But that's not big enough,' said Collins, a look of puzzlement on her face. 'Men don't have shoes that small or that shape.'

'No, they don't,' said the forensic officer. 'This is a woman's shoe print; there are a number of them around the body and leading from the door to here and then back to the door. There are only one set of shoe prints and they are more pronounced on the way in, so its safe to assume that one woman has carried the other, probably over her shoulder judging by the irregular prints, and set her down by the pillar to tie her up.'

Collins shook her head in disbelief; she hadn't even considered the possibility that a woman could be responsible for the murders and now she was thrown totally off balance. Was it possible that in looking for a man they had been thinking on the wrong track all this time? She could see the footprints clearly now and it was obvious that there were no other prints around the body other than the soft smudges left by the forensic peoples' shoe protectors. This was unexpected but it was the first piece of solid evidence they had collected; it wasn't much but it changed the picture completely. The known male weirdos and perverts could be discounted now. According to Dr. Davies the chances of a woman carrying out this sort of murder was virtually zero. There were far fewer known dangerous women to look for than men, a fact which could narrow the search dramatically. Collins had the first feelings of optimism she had felt in a long time.

Chapter Eight

James had arrived at work early on Monday morning. His fear was preventing him going into a deep sleep and he was looking very haggard, appearing to have aged. As he stared into the mirror in the washroom at the lab, he hardly recognised himself; his face was gaunt and his eyes were puffy and dark underneath. He felt like he hadn't slept for weeks, which was probably not far from the truth. He washed his face and walked down the corridor to Dr Davies's office.

After a short time in the waiting area the secretary summoned him to the office, where Davies was just finishing off a phone conversation. He waited patiently as the doctor ended the call and greeted him.

'Good morning, James; how are you today?'

He was slightly irritated; couldn't Davies tell by looking at him how he was? He hid his frustration and replied as politely as he could.

'Well, Doctor, I wish I could tell you I was well but I'm afraid the nightmares are becoming worse and I haven't slept properly for days now.'

Davies studied his face for a few moments and could see that his colleague was indeed looking more distressed. He was obviously having a hard time coping judging by the dark rings around his eyes. Davies decided to put James in a semi-hypnotic trance in order to delve more deeply into his mind and see where the problem lay. Things like this often came from some bad experience a person may have had in their childhood. Repressed memories could take years to come to the surface of a person's consciousness; it was the brain's way of protecting the mind from extreme trauma, but in some cases it caused problems and that was where Davies came in. People with these sorts of problems often ended up on his consulting couch; he would usually have a few sessions, identify the problem, and encourage the patient to recognise their fears and the reasons for them. They were often like phobias, totally irrational but so real to the person who was suffering from them. He hoped he could help James; he seemed like a pleasant young man and was well thought of by his colleagues, who considered him to be bright and conscientious in his work with a very easy-going, carefree disposition.

Davies waited until James had relaxed a little in the reclining chair before he commenced his hypnosis technique. He soon had James in a dreamy state and began probing into his mind, first letting him ramble on with incoherent thoughts, and then beginning to ask questions to build up a clearer picture of what was going on in there. James described his dreams in more detail than he remembered in his conscious state. Davies found himself becoming more concerned as James continued his account of his dreams. These weren't normal dream events, not with the graphic detail that was emerging; it was almost as though James were giving a commentary of actual events.

Davies remembered a case he had worked on eighteen months ago in the United States where he had interviewed a man in very similar circumstances to James's. The subject in that case had gone to the police, so great was his concern that he was actually committing murder in his sleeping hours. After hours of consultations and questioning, an investigation had been started; this had resulted in the finding of five bodies. The location had been described by the subject in such detail that the detectives working on the case were convinced that the subject was the killer of the five missing persons, who had ended up murdered and buried under a floor of a private house in the middle of an affluent area just outside of New York City.

As the investigation continued, however, with the questioning of the property owner, it was quickly established that the subject had never actually left his home state of Georgia. The investigation team, including Davies, had turned their attention to the home owner, who at first seemed the model citizen. But as they dug deeper into his past they realised that here was a very sick individual. He had been expelled from school for torturing and killing a school pet rabbit, a classic trait in psychopathic behaviour. There were further records of his sadistic behaviour in his younger days and then nothing for years after that. He was one who had slipped through the net; these people could be very clever if they realised they were in danger of losing the liberty to continue the life they led. He seemed to have changed his habits to become a decent, law abiding citizen, gaining good qualifications, getting a good career, and living a seemingly normal life. But, as Davies knew, he was like a time bomb waiting to go off. Nobody knew yet what triggered these episodes but the effects were devastating. After his arrest the evidence was uncovered, and eventually the subject who had led them to these horrific murders was exonerated and cleared of any involvement whatsoever in the murders.

The homeowner had been duly convicted in a court of law and was now interred in the state prison, awaiting execution. The sad part of that case was that the innocent party in the affair had lost his mind completely; he couldn't cope with the recurring nightmares and had slipped into a stupor from which there appeared to be no escape. Davies hoped the similarities in James's case were just coincidental. Knowing someone as a colleague made it more personal and he would hate to see James end up the same way as that poor soul had in the American case, locked forever in a state of torment, his mind shut down to all reality.

Davies brought James out of his trance slowly to try lessening the trauma he may feel. Although he was sweating profusely, he didn't appear as disturbed as he had seemed at the previous session. Davies would remember that for his next consultation; it would appear that the deeper the trance, the fewer traumas were suffered on waking.

Chapter Nine

Andrea Collins had just finished an interview and was as excited as she could get over a murder case. Her forensic team had found a human hair fibre at the murder scene that didn't belong to the victim; it was being tested at the lab. She had also gained solid information from two witnesses. It had quickly been established that the victim, Sam, had been out with two girlfriends for a nights' dancing in the city centre and Collins had just finished interviewing the second girl. Her story tallied exactly with the first girls' statement and there was no reason to suspect any of them were involved in the killing. Both seemed in genuine states of shock and grief but had bravely told their stories in a clear and concise way.

They were both relatively sober on that night, so they were quite clear when relating the events leading to their friend's death. They had told Collins that Sam preferred women to men, sexually. That was something the family hadn't told her team, and perhaps they hadn't known. Collins wondered if this had any significance in the light that they were now looking for a woman. They had gone on to describe how Sam had met and danced with a very attractive brunette, before returning to their table to retrieve her bag and coat. She was excited and in an excellent mood, and she had promised to meet them for lunch on Monday and tell them all about her new friend. She had said goodnight and left the nightclub they were in, arm in arm with her new acquaintance.

Her name, they said, was Jayne. Sam had told them when she came to collect her coat. Collins wondered if that was the killer's first mistake; maybe she had thought the girl was alone and so an easier target. Most of the other victims had been missing persons, runaways, and usually without family or friends. Many of them had been found to have drink or drugs related health problems at the post mortem examinations and that could also have some bearing on the case.

Collins was in buoyant mood, but she needed to sit down and go over all the files again to see if things looked any different now they were looking for a woman. It could be that simple, she thought; if your mind was so focused in one direction you could be looking right at some important piece of information and not realise the significance of what you were looking at, because it didn't fit in with your train of thought.

She left instructions for her team to follow and found her driver, Paul. They left Sheffield in the early evening, Collins making notes on the journey back; she had to speak to Davies again. The profile he was building for her was assuming they were looking for a male and based on the outdated information she had provided him with. She would now have to divulge all that the files contained to him in order to have him make a proper evaluation, something she had foolishly been reluctant to do. It was also time to call Kate Mitchell and leak a little information through the press.

She called Davies and arranged to meet him the following morning. Luckily he was in town to attend a seminar, and he would have an hour to spare her first thing in the morning. Next she called Mitchell to arrange a face to face, something she didn't like to do but felt was crucial to the investigation. She would have to base what she told Mitchell on whatever she could learn from Davies.

Collins had her mind in overdrive. Everything had happened so fast over the last twenty four hours, her head was spinning with an overload of information. She needed to get home, shower, eat, and relax. Perhaps then she could begin to formulate some plan of action. Her eyes closed and she drifted into a half sleep for the rest of the journey home, only waking when her driver informed her that they had arrived.

She closed and locked the front door behind her. Undressing and leaving her clothes where they lay, she made her way to the bathroom and ran herself a hot bath. She sank into the hot foamy water, laying back, stretching her weary limbs as she sipped at a glass of red wine. Her eyes opened and she cursed at the clock, which showed she had been asleep for over an hour. The food would have to wait, she thought, as she towelled herself off and collapsed, exhausted, into bed.

Chapter Ten

Collins woke at 7 a.m. as was her custom. She felt as though she hadn't slept for a week and was absolutely ravenous. She made herself a pot of strong coffee and warmed a couple of croissants. That would give her the start she needed for the day; she had always been a believer in eating breakfast. She laughed at herself in the mirror over the breakfast bar. I'm getting such an old bore, she thought, living here alone, no visitors or friends to speak of, just an occasional visit from a work colleague. She was approaching forty years old; her marriage had ended over ten years before. Work had got in the way, but now she was feeling that she needed to share her life with somebody. She promised herself again that when this case was over, she would definitely start living a bit more.

She left her apartment and walked the short distance to the university faculty where her meeting with Davies was to take place. She arrived just before nine, right at the same time as Davies. They greeted each other and made their way to a spare office, which the dean had kindly made available for their use.

Collins got straight to the point. There wasn't much time to speak with Davies, and she needed him to be fully briefed before the meeting was finished.

'There has been another killing. Same M.O., definitely not copycat, the same weapon as was used for the last four killings. We are now looking for a woman. We have a name, we have foot prints from the crime scene, and we have witnesses who saw the latest victim leaving a nightclub with the suspect. We have people working on a photofit image, based on descriptions given by two witnesses. We also have a hair sample; the forensic boys found it after we left the scene.'

'You have been busy since the last time we spoke,' said Davies. 'You're sure it's a woman?'

'Forensic are sure. The only footprints around the body were women's shoes. They traced the steps and were clear that the victim was carried into the building by the person wearing those shoes. That fits in with our statements from the witnesses who saw their friend leave the club with a woman.'

Davies removed his glasses and rubbed his temples slowly.

'Well, I have to say, this is very unusual, though not unheard of. I am afraid I have been guilty of making assumptions based on my previous experiences. My apologies. I can assure you I will be more diligent in future; that is, if you still wish me to assist you.'

'Of course, Doctor. We all made the same assumptions about the killer being a man; it's too easy to fall into a routine of stereotyping people. I should be the one apologising, I should have known better than to think in straight lines.'

Collins reached into her briefcase and removed a thick manila file which contained the details of each and every murder in the series. She handed it over to Davies.

'This is everything we have, Doctor; please read it, and see if you can make any sense out of these killings.'

Davies took the file and flicked through the pages. 'I don't think we will ever make sense of these sorts of killings,' he said. He studied a page and then returned to a previous page as though he had seen something important. Collins waited with as much patience as she could muster, watching Davies intently as he flicked through a few pages and then went back over them. Finally he closed the folder and stood up.

'I wish you had shown me this file sooner, Detective. We have a collector here. I would guess that somewhere there is a room full of trophies; that is how the killer will view them. The killings are getting more regular. That could mean that the collector may be nearing a peak, achieving a goal almost. The killings could stop altogether when that goal is reached.'

'What, just stop?' asked Collins, a look of disbelief on her face.

'It's a possibility, Andrea; we don't understand how the mind of a psychopath works. They can just switch off one day and live a perfectly normal life, seemingly oblivious to anything they have done.'

'So you're telling me that our killer could just disappear, just go back to a normal life, as though nothing had happened?'

'It is a possibility, yes. We really need to discuss this further but unfortunately we are out of time. Give me a couple of days to go over the file and see if I can form some sort of profile. I'll call you when I have something for you and arrange to meet you. It would help to see your operations room to get a feel for the case, if that would be possible.'

'Yes, certainly Doctor, thank you for your time. If you need any further information please don't hesitate to call me at any time, day or night.'

Collins left the building and walked down the High Street deep in thought. This was really far more complicated than she had imagined. It was worrying because she felt slightly out of her depth. She needed to study all the information she could find on this subject and she desperately needed more time with Davies.

The day was bright and sunny but there was still a chill in the air. Collins found a café and ordered herself a nice hot pot of coffee. She sat for half an hour, sipping her drink and watching the world pass by. If only her life was as uncomplicated as theirs, she thought, as she stared through the window at the contented looking people in the streets. They were all going about their business without a care in the world.

She paid her bill and walked along the pavement towards her apartment, through the bustle of the shoppers and office workers. She let herself in and settled into her one luxury, an old leather armchair. It had cost her a fortune a few years before, but she still considered it the best buy she had ever made. Three hours before her meeting with Mitchell, she thought, stretching her legs out and closing her eyes. She was asleep in seconds, exhaustion finally taking its toll.

Chapter Eleven

The door bell rang just as Collins stepped out of the shower. This would be Mitchell, she thought, as she quickly threw on a bath robe before going down the stairs to open the door.

'Good afternoon Andrea, how are you today?' asked Mitchell.

'How do I look?' replied Collins.

Mitchell laughed. 'Do you really want me to tell you, Andrea?'

Collins had to smile. Kate Mitchell was one of those people whose gusto for life was infectious. She would always be the one to liven the party up, thought Collins; with her good looks and bubbly personality she couldn't fail to cheer people up.

'Give me five minutes to make myself look human. Help yourself to drinks,' she called over her shoulder.

'Take as long as you need,' Kate shouted after her with a mischievous smile on her face.

She looked around the room at the sparse furnishing, nodding her head and smiling to herself. This was almost a carbon copy of her own apartment; just the bare essentials, and no signs of a man living here. She guessed correctly that Andrea only used this place like you would use a hotel. Like her own, Andrea's life revolved around work. There would be no time for romance or socialising, maybe an occasional fling with someone from work but they never lasted. In any case, that sort of affair interfered with your career and nothing could come between an ambitious woman and her career.

Kate Mitchell was a couple of years younger than Andrea and she too was in excellent shape, with good looks and a figure to match. Neither of them looked their age she thought as she looked in the mirror hanging over the fireplace. She wondered if either of them would ever lose the drive and ambition, maybe find a man and settle down to a quiet, stress-free life. Hers was a restless life; although gaining great personal satisfaction from her career achievements she knew she would always strive for more and knew that as long as she pursued that course she would never find real happiness. But could she ever be happy without her career? She doubted it. Maybe people like her and Andrea were just destined to be alone.

Andrea entered the room, towelling her hair dry; she sat at the table opposite where Kate had taken a seat.

'We need to think about putting a news article out as soon as possible, Kate; our killer is becoming more prolific. We need to stop her before she kills again, or disappears altogether.'

Kate blinked and looked at Andrea's face. She had just heard her partner (that was how she was beginning to think of Andrea) use feminine terms to describe the killer. She was surprised; weren't serial killers always men?

'So you have a lead, then?'

'Well, we have a couple of leads, Kate; nothing really solid yet, but as you have probably guessed from what I've just said we are now looking for a female in connection with our murders.'

She looked at Kate and decided to tell all. She felt she could trust her to co-operate fully.

'We have witnesses who saw the latest victim leaving a nightclub with a female. Before she left the club the dead girl told her friends that the suspect was called Jayne.'

Kate's interest was aroused now. Although she had spoken to Collins a few times over the phone, nothing much had happened of any importance. This was more like it, she thought.

'You must have more, Andrea; being seen with someone doesn't make you a killer. Other than that, what makes you think it's a woman who's doing the killing?'

'The crime scene was a disused warehouse,' Collins explained to Mitchell, 'and no-one had been in there for months. There was a heavy layer of dust on the floor; the forensic people were able to get a clear picture of all the movements in the place from the footprints.'

Mitchell had her notebook out and was scribbling furiously; for some reason she had never been able to master shorthand.

'So you're telling me that it was a woman's footprint?'

'Absolutely positive. One woman carried the other over her shoulder into the building, tied her to a pillar, and then killed her. The tracks on the way out were a lot lighter and more evenly balanced, because the killer didn't have such a weight on her shoulder when she made her exit.'

'She must have been a big woman to carry that sort of weight, mustn't she?'

'Not necessarily, according to our psychiatrist. Apparently, these people can have almost superhuman strength as part of their disorder. They can be very slight in stature but still have enormous strength, so much that it could take five or six men to restrain them. We are talking about a very dangerous person here, Kate.'

'Well I figured that one out for myself when you told me she likes to cut heads off, Andrea.'

'Ok, I apologise for that, I've got my teacher's head on. You wouldn't believe how dim some of my colleagues are. I often think I'm talking to children when I try to explain some things to them.'

Kate laughed rather nervously. This was getting scary; she had never been involved this closely in a murder investigation, and certainly not one involving a serial killer.

'No problem, Andrea; I feel the same when I talk to my Editor sometimes.' She took a sip of her drink. 'So, what do you mean when you say the killer might disappear?'

'We have a psychiatrist working on the case; he's putting together a profile for us. He says that psychopaths are very unpredictable. They may just stop killing altogether when they have had enough. They are totally irrational sometimes, but coldly calculating at others. There's just no telling what might be the next move she makes.'

'So how the hell are you going to catch her?'

'If I had a crystal ball I'd tell you, Kate; but seriously, that's where you come in. I want you to release some information in your next edition. We have to be very careful what we put out but we need to put some pressure on. This sort of killer can be very egotistical; if we can hit the right notes we may be able to provoke her into making a mistake.'

'Or provoke her into killing again?'

'Maybe, but if it leads to an arrest and gets the killer behind bars where she belongs, that is the price we'll have to pay.'

Mitchell shuddered at the thought. The price another poor girl will have to pay, more likely; not Andrea. She would be alive and get the credit for the arrest and probably a promotion as well. Mitchell was glad she was a journalist; she didn't think she could take the sort of calculated decisions which could lead to another human being losing their life in such a horrific way. It was clear that Collins was prepared to do just such a thing; the ends justified the means was obviously her view and, although Mitchell baulked at the very idea, she could see the logic in it.

The two of them spent nearly another hour discussing the case in great detail. They agreed on the story that Kate would run in her newspaper, providing of course that the editor agreed to print. Mitchell was sure there wouldn't be a problem; what editor in their right mind would miss such an opportunity? She made a call to her office to tell them she had a major breaking story so they could hold space for her.

The two women shook hands and agreed to speak again the next day; Mitchell walked quickly to the taxi rank and ordered the driver to take her to the newspaper's offices. She would normally walk the mile or so, but she had a very busy day ahead of her and didn't want to waste a minute of it.

Chapter Twelve

After finishing his lectures early, Davies had driven to his home. It was a three-bedroomed cottage set in its own small plot, just far enough out of town to enjoy the luxuries and conveniences of both city and rural living. He was in his study, his favourite room in the cottage. It was lined with bookcases which were overflowing; everywhere around the room were files and more books, stacked in uneven piles wherever there was a space left to put them.

This was his place for relaxing; he had lived alone since his wife had died, and never really took an interest in the opposite sex anymore unless it was professional. He wasn't unattractive; he was six feet one and very fit for his sixty one years, and he was what people usually referred to as ruggedly handsome. But after thirty five years with the same partner he didn't really want to start over again and was happy with his memories of a wonderful relationship. The study was also where he did most of his work, spending endless hours poring over files, documents and numerous books.

He was reading a file now, the file that Collins had given him that morning; he had read it more than once already but was drawn to its contents like a magnet.

When he had flicked through the file at his meeting with

Collins, his mind had immediately registered the manner of the killings and the way that the victims' heads had disappeared, along with their hearts. It was like deja-vous; he was certain he had seen some of these details before, only days previously. He had tried to hide his disquiet from Collins, but his mind was thinking back to the last consultation he had undertaken, and to the notes he had written. Some of the details he was reading could have been taken directly from his own notes, they were so similar. He was deeply disturbed; that consultation had been with his colleague, James Elliot.

This case bore striking similarities to the one in New York which had left such a lasting impression on him, mainly because it had proved to him that humans could have a psychic link with one another. James Elliot was having dreams just the same way as the main suspect had in that case. Davies remembered the way that the suspect had ended up in a padded cell, locked away for his own safety. Even though he was innocent of any crime, the terror of his nightmares had driven him to a complete mental breakdown, from which he would probably never recover.

He had to get James back into his consultation room as soon as possible. He needed to try and coax some information from him. This could, of course, be pure coincidence; but he had an awful feeling that he was becoming involved in a very frightening series of events and he dreaded to think where they may lead. There was also the question of client confidentiality. James was his client and he could not, under any circumstances, go against his oaths as a doctor. To reveal any part of clients' records would be in breach of the ethics of his profession. He also had a duty, both as a member of the investigation team and as a citizen, to do all he could to assist in the arrest of a mass murderer. He needed to give this some extremely careful thought, and much of that thinking would be based on what information he could glean from his client at their next consultation.

Chapter Thirteen

The morning edition of Kate Mitchell's newspaper was selling like hot cakes; none of the other papers had heard so much as a whisper about this story. For once, a newspaper claiming an exclusive story really did have something no one else had.

Kate Mitchell was basking in the glory; she had worked hard until late at night to polish up the detail of her article, and had just made the deadline in time for publication.

She had arrived at the office early to find a copy of the early edition on her desk. Her colleagues were now crowding round her, congratulating her on the scoop and asking all sorts of questions. She was surprised to find she had mixed feelings; she felt the warm glow of satisfaction that comes with the plaudits, but she also felt distinctly uneasy. Here was everybody congratulating her for her wonderful job, while a few miles away, a young girl was lying in a hospital morgue, her life ended violently and tragically early.

She felt her face flushing, suddenly angry at both herself and her colleagues. What had this job done to them all? All that mattered was that their paper had the exclusive. Had they all become so cold and callous? Not a thought spared for the victims, just the smug, self-satisfied back slapping, as though they had won the lottery. She suddenly hated her job and hated herself; she was beginning to feel slightly nauseous.

She was saved by the editor. He called her into his office before she had time to boil over and let her anger show. She sat in the chair opposite her boss and looked at him, hoping she wasn't going to hear more of what she had just heard from her colleagues. She needn't have worried; the editor was one of the old school of journalists. He still had codes of conduct that the younger generation of news people didn't seem to understand, or maybe just chose to ignore. You had to have ethics and rules to follow; respect was a word that they didn't seem to have learned, and self respect was totally alien to their way of thinking. Who cared what people may think about you, as long as you got the job done? It didn't matter; the ends justified the means. Well not always, thought the editor.

He was studying Mitchell closely; he had been watching her from his office and had seen her becoming more uncomfortable. He was a good judge of character and had always regarded Mitchell as someone with integrity. He had guessed rightly the reasons for her discomfort, and summoned her to his office before she blew her top.

'Well Kate, you seem to have hit the bull's-eye this time. I've just had the Chief Constable of Sheffield on the phone, screaming about irresponsible reporters. That tells me that your story is completely accurate. He wants to know who leaked.'

'You know better than that, boss. I have an insider at the heart of the investigation and you know I would never compromise them.'

She was careful, even in this office, not to reveal whether her source was male or female. Her boss nodded.

'I know, Kate; I wouldn't even ask. I want you to run with this story. You can have whatever resources you need, just make sure you keep me up to speed with any new developments.'

'Yes sir, thank you, I will.'

'Just one more thing, Kate. I know this one has hit hard. When you see the details of these girls' deaths, and look at the photographs of their broken bodies, you begin to question your role as a journalist. But you do have a role, Kate; and you need to carry on playing that role. Always remember that, above all else, you're a servant of the public. You're doing a good job Kate, and you're doing it for the right reasons.'

Mitchell was glad that her boss seemed to understand her feelings. She stood to leave.

'Thanks boss, I needed that pep talk,' she said with a half-smile. 'I'll keep you informed.'

She left the editor's office and returned to her own desk. The excitement had died down now and she was able to collect her notes and her copy of the morning edition without arousing too much attention.

She left the office hurriedly, making her way to a small coffee bar around the corner which she used when she needed a little peace and quiet. She ordered her drink and sat at a table at the back of the bar, where she could spread out the paper and read her story. The headline screamed from the front page:

'HEAD HUNTER ON THE LOOSE' Exclusive from Kate Mitchell.

Her journalistic instincts took over her thinking; this was what people like her worked for, to see their names under this sort of headline. This could be an award winning story for her; she thought again of the picture of the last victim. Strung from a pillar, her head missing, and her heart ripped from her body. She quickly came back down to earth. She read through the article, checking the details were correct and that there were no changes to her original text; she hated having someone alter her work. She took great pride in her writing skills and was always insulted when someone saw fit to change it. There were no alterations; it was exactly as she had penned it the night before. The report gave details of the last killing and suggested there could be up to five more victims.

She had agreed with Andrea not to reveal the full extent of the injuries inflicted on the victims. Collins would be inundated with calls from the public, offering all sorts of information. Some would claim that the strange man next door to them was the killer; others would claim to be the killer, some even coming forward to confess. Every call had to be followed up, because somewhere in those claims and allegations could be the truth. It would be painstaking work; endless hours of filing reports, then cross-referencing every single one to try and find just a single clue. The public didn't realise just how many crimes were actually solved after the police had received information from sources other than detective work. Probably the majority of prosecutions resulted directly from information supplied by a member of the general public. By not revealing all of the details of the murders, they would be able to discount most of the false claims of responsibility within hours of receiving them. They could then get down to the serious business of sifting through the rest of the data, in the hope that the breakthrough they needed was contained somewhere within. In the story which was printed that morning, Mitchell had told how the victims had been found with their heads severed and with knife wounds to the bodies. She hadn't included the facts that both the hearts and heads had been severed and taken from the crime scene. She had talked in brutal terms of the person that had perpetrated these crimes, calling them twisted and cowardly, scornful of their weakness in picking the most vulnerable of people as victims. There were no punches pulled in her attack on the killer's character; it was hoped that these words might provoke a reaction of some sort from this twisted individual.

She finished reading the story and was satisfied with her work. She drank the last of her coffee and made her way from the bar onto the street, where she hailed a black cab to take her the couple of miles to her apartment. A few hours' rest was called for; she needed to stay fresh and alert if she wanted to be of any help to Andrea.

Chapter Fourteen

Amy had woken from a deep sleep not long after James had gone to bed. She wandered into the kitchen to make coffee, where she found the copy of James's daily newspaper on the table. She stopped in front of the table, looking down at the headline. So they had finally found out, she thought as she read through the article. She wondered why the police had never released any information about her quest; maybe because if the public found out what an incompetent bunch of fools they were, they would all be sacked.

There was a small picture of Kate Mitchell under the credits and Amy studied it closely. This bitch wanted to stop her quest; she could tell by the hysterical way the article was written. Didn't she realise how important the collection was? She would have to keep an eye on this bitch, she thought; some of these reporters could be very tenacious. She didn't want a nosey, jumped up bitch like this Mitchell woman ruining her plans. Amy went to the drawer in the sideboard where she kept her scissors. She took the front page of the newspaper and carefully cut out the picture of Mitchell. She held it up to study it more closely; yes, she thought, a vindictive bitch. Well, she had better watch where she was sticking her nose because nothing and nobody was going to stop Amy in her quest.

Amy slipped out of the back door and walked around to her car. She had spotted a nice looking piece during the day, while out shopping. The piece had been with two friends and had been discussing where they were going this very night; they were meeting with a dozen more friends, for a hen party they had said. One of them was to be married the following week, and the girls were planning a wild night of fun in a local night club. It wasn't really in Amy's area; it would disrupt her pattern but she was angry and was going to teach the Mitchell bitch a lesson. She would be sorry when she saw the results of her interference.

Amy arrived at the club and went straight to the bar where she ordered herself a soft drink. She stood at the bar and chatted to a couple of people who were also waiting for friends. As she chatted her eyes were scanning the room for the piece she had seen earlier. Nearly half an hour had passed and Amy was beginning to get restless. What a disappointment, she thought; that piece had been a real stunner and would have fit in nicely between her two favourites, a striking looking blonde and a gorgeous redhead.

Amy was just about to start looking for another suitable piece when there was a commotion at the entrance and in trooped her piece with a large group of friends. They were all scantily clad and quite obviously enjoying all the attention they were drawing from the rest of the club goers, They were also quite tipsy by the way they were behaving and that suited Amy just fine. She made her way to the dance floor where she began her polished routine of seduction. If that didn't work she would just befriend her, it didn't matter what the method was, as long as the goal was achieved.

The girls were smoking joints, hiding them clumsily under the tables. That gave Amy her way in; she had been dancing with her piece and some of the others and now quietly asked her if she would like something with a little more kick.

'Sure, I'm up for it,' the piece slurred. Her name was Julie; she hadn't collected a Julie before. It was lovely to have new names for her display. Amy suggested going to the washroom, away from prying eyes, and Julie readily agreed, following

Amy across the floor and into the toilet area. Amy had bought a drink with her and had put the sedative into the glass; she gave the piece a small pill that was nothing more than an aspirin and then handed her the glass to wash the pill down. Julie was thirsty and drank it all while Amy watched her with anticipation.

'I could do with a bit of fresh air, I'm feeling a little dizzy,' slurred Amy, pushing open the crash bar on the fire exit leading to the back street where she had parked her car earlier on. Julie followed and leaned against the wall next to Amy.

'That was strong stuff, I feel like I'm floating,' she whispered. She was giggling and slowly loosing consciousness. Amy caught her before she slid to the floor, hefting her easily over her shoulder. She looked down the street to make sure no one had seen them, and then walked the few yards to her car. She opened the boot with her key fob and dumped Julie in a heap into the boot space. She had to fold her legs underneath her to fit her in properly; then, throwing in Julie's bag after her, she locked the boot and went around to start the car.

Within minutes she had arrived at the place she had located for the ritual, an old barn down a country lane. There wasn't much left of the walls; just enough ceiling beams to get the ropes secured, ready to fasten around Julie's wrists. Amy tied her piece to the beam and cut away her upper clothing; she cut a strip from the tee shirt and tied it around Julie's mouth. She placed her holdall next to her as she looked at her watch; five minutes and the piece would regain consciousness. Amy felt the rush of excitement flowing through her body; she could barely contain herself as she watched the girl's face intently for the first signs of fear. Amy's face was a picture of serenity as she waited with growing anticipation for the wakening.

Chapter Fifteen

James was looking at the girl. She was tied by her wrists to the timber beams over her head, and she was beginning to stir. He could see the stars clearly through the roof where it had rotted away; it looked like an old barn or outbuilding. The moonlight was playing down across the girl's face, creating an eerie picture of light and shadow. He could see the holdall to his side; he had seen that holdall before, he knew, somewhere in another dream.

He wondered what he was doing here. Why was this girl tied, half naked, from the roof beams? He moved to help her, to undo her bonds; instead his hands went to the holdall. He reached inside and felt cold steel. His hands came out of the holdall with a massive serrated knife and a butcher's type meat cleaver. His mind was telling him to put the implements back in the bag and release the girl, but he had no control over his actions. He looked down at his hands and was confused even more. They were someone else's hands, smaller and more slender than his own; they were a woman's hands. The girl had woken up now and was staring at him with fear and panic in her eyes; he wanted to take the gag from around her mouth and release her but was powerless. He felt himself smiling at her as she began to sob, her cries muffled by the cloth tied around her mouth.

He was talking to the girl, calling her Julie, reassuring her; the words were jumbled and it wasn't his voice. It was a woman's voice, one that sounded familiar, but he couldn't place it. It was surreal; he was here watching this scene unfold, seeing through someone else's eyes, but unable to influence the events taking place right before him. He was becoming agitated; a feeling of dread was invading his mind as images of past dreams flicked through his consciousness. He saw the feet moving slowly towards the girl, he knew they weren't his own feet, he could see the women's shoes on them. He watched as she struggled violently to free herself; she was helpless, her eyes wide and staring in horror at the knife he was lifting towards her body. He could hear the garbled words coming from his mouth, soothing, calm, and somehow strangely relaxing.

He watched his arm extend, the knife pointing towards the girl's chest at a point just under her breastbone and to the left. The smell was foul; he realised the girl had emptied her bowels as she saw the knife coming towards her body. He watched in horror as the hand pushed the knife slowly into the girl's body, not stopping until it was buried to the hilt. His mind was reeling; he wanted to stop this madness. Instead he watched as his hand grabbed the still-conscious girl by the hair and yanked her head back to expose her throat. His other hand came up as if in slow motion and arced through the air, the gleam of the moonlight catching on the metal of the cleaver as it sailed surely towards its target; the defenceless throat of the terrified, already dying girl.

The blood spurted in jets from the girl's severed jugular; the cleaver rose and fell again and again. The sickening sound of the cleaver as it cut into flesh and sinew and crushed bone made the bile rise in his throat. With a final blow the head was severed and jerked into the air in his hand as it separated from the neck. He held the head in front of his face, staring back at the lifeless eyes of the dead girl. His mind cried out for release from this nightmare but he couldn't break the spell. He recoiled as he watched the hand drop the head into the holdall and take hold of the knife, still protruding from the chest.

He saw the gold wedding band on the slender finger of the hand as it started sawing and hacking at the chest, opening it up until there was room to reach in and grab the heart tightly. Pulling taut against the connecting tubes, the knife did its evil work, slicing through tissue easily and cleanly. The heart came away in the hand; it was raised before his eyes and then dropped into the holdall along with the head. His head was swimming, his vision blurred; things were becoming hazy and distant, and he could hear a voice, laughing and hysterical.

There was movement, just a blur, he felt he was moving quickly. The light grew in strength; he had the impression of being out side, the moon shining more brightly. There was a car. He saw the boot open and the holdall thrown in. Why was Amy's car here? he thought vaguely, his mind not making any sense or order of the events. He was behind the wheel of the car, driving fast. He was sure he recognised the road as the A34. After speeding along for a short time it turned into a side road which ended in a dirt track. It was a long driveway; he watched in detached fascination as the car drove up to what appeared to be a farmhouse, with a large barn built to one side. He was out of the car, at the door, down the steps under the trapdoor; back in the room from his dreams, the single light swinging from its flex.

His vision was clearing, his eyes regaining their focus. He looked around the room, and all he could see was dark shapes along the walls. He moved closer and the shapes slowly became heads, eyes staring at him. He was going mad; the eyes were accusing him, pleading with him.

He didn't know where he was and he didn't know why he was here or why he was seeing things through these accursed eyes. 'Let me go!' his mind was screaming.

'Hello Amy.'

His head turned slowly to the centre of the shelves which adorned the walls of the cellar. There was the urn with the painted eyes, looking directly at him; he felt his mouth open and heard the shrill, manic tones of a frightened female voice emanating from it.

'Hello Mother, look what I've brought for you!'

He saw the hand reach into the holdall and lift the head out, holding it up towards the urn. He placed the head on the table in front of the urn, aware of those evil-looking eyes that seemed to see right into his head. He was sure they knew what he was thinking; they were mocking and cruel. He reached down into the bag at his feet, feeling the warm stickiness of the heart as his hand lifted it upwards to hold it in front of the urn. His hand moved towards his mouth, he felt his mouth open and tasted the blood soaked heart as it touched his lips. His teeth sank into the heart, and his mind finally released him from the horror.

James's eyes clicked open. He was back in his bedroom, and the moonlight cast soft shadows across the walls. He was still seeing images even though he was awake; just flashes, jumbled thoughts mixed with fleeting images of headless bodies. The bloodied hearts kept flashing before his eyes. He saw the cleaver swinging through the air as he had in his dream, he saw the eyes, there seemed to be hundreds of them. Staring, silent, dead, all of them except for the ones on the vase; they were very alive, blazing with anger and hatred, seeming to pierce his very soul.

He couldn't stand it any longer; jumping up from the bed he ran to the bathroom and turned on the shower. He ran the water cold and stood under the freezing spray, his mind numb with fear, horror, and revulsion. His thoughts slowly began to clear; the flow of water had turned his body icily cold. He was shivering, unsure whether it was from the cold or the fear. He stepped from the shower, threw on his bathrobe, and made his way downstairs to the kitchen, checking that Amy was still sleeping on his way through the bedroom.

James made himself coffee, strong and black. He really couldn't go on like this, it was destroying his life. Glancing in the mirror he was shocked. His face had become gaunter, his eyes were puffy and black underneath; he looked years older than he was. Maybe it was time to talk to Amy about his nightmares. First he would see Davies again to discuss the reasons for his dreams. There must be an explanation; he would demand that Davies help him quickly before he lost his mind altogether. He was coming apart at the seams and he was unable to prevent it happening. He was sure Davies would understand.

James sat at the kitchen table, drinking coffee, listening to the radio, not daring to go to sleep again. He sat there for two hours until it was time to dress for work. He left the house quietly, careful not to wake Amy, and drove along the country lanes, trying to focus on the work he needed to do in the lab. If he kept his mind busy he might not get the images recurring like they had been. He arrived at the centre and immediately went to see Dr Davies's secretary to arrange a consultation for that morning.

Chapter Sixteen

Kate Mitchell had been in the office for an hour, writing up a couple of articles she had left to one side for a few days. They seemed trivial compared to the story she had broken in her front page exclusive. Her phone was buzzing constantly and beginning to annoy her; she sighed and picked it up.

'Hello, Mitchell here,' she said testily. The girl on the switch informed her that she had a call from a member of the public who wanted to pass on some information.

'Would you like to take the call?' asked the girl.

Mitchell nearly told the switch to hold all calls, but calmed down enough to act professionally and ask who was calling. She had received hundreds of calls from people claiming to know or be the killer, and she was tired of the time-wasting. These people were as sick as the killer, rubbernecks intent on their five minutes of fame. They would claim to be the devil himself if it got their name in the papers.

'Okay, ask who is calling,' she said to the switch.

'She says her name is Jayne and you will know who she is,' spoke the voice on the other end of the line.

It took a few seconds for the words to register with Mitchell. She wasn't properly focused this morning; her mind was jumping from one subject to another. She felt her heart miss a beat as she heard the name. The hair stood up on the back of her neck; surely it couldn't be the killer? But they hadn't released that information in the story. Coincidence? But why had the caller said that she would know who she was? She suddenly felt cold; her arms had gone goosy, and she could feel her stomach knotting up. She took a deep breath, trying to keep her voice as normal as possible, but she could hear the strain as she told the switch girl to put the caller through.

'Hello, this is Mitchell, who am I speaking to?'

'Hello Kate Mitchell. I'm Jayne, you know me.'

'I'm sorry; I don't know anyone called Jayne. What exactly do you want?'

'Don't play games with me, Kate; her friends must have told the police my name, and your friend Detective Collins must have told you.'

'Whose friends are you talking about, Jayne?'

'The bitch in Sheffield, as you well know.'

Mitchell felt her blood run cold. Her hands were shaking; it took an enormous effort to get her words out.

'Why are you doing this, Jayne? Those girls didn't deserve to die.'

'Oh, they didn't die, Kate. They're all part of me, all alive and well and living with me and Mother.'

The voice was cold and detached, talking about the victims as though they were talking about the price of groceries. Mitchell was chilled to the bone, her heart was pounding in her chest, she was sure that this was the killer and she wanted to find out why she was carrying out these atrocious crimes. Her journalistic instincts had kicked in and she wanted to ask all sorts of questions. Her excitement overruled her good sense; she should have put the caller on hold, tried to get a recording and reach Collins, but the opportunity was too good to miss. She was sure Collins would understand.

'Tell me why you killed them, Jayne.'

The voice came back on the line.

'Why are you insulting me Kate? You weren't very nice to me when you wrote your story.'

Mitchell's thoughts were racing; she didn't want to lose the caller before she could interrogate her, and so she decided to take a softer stance.

'I'm sorry Jayne, but my boss wanted to sensationalise the story. I would never insult you like that, but I was ordered to. I can't afford to lose my job. I think I can help you if you just trust me.'

There was a pause and then came the most chilling sound of laughter she had ever heard. It was manic, and Mitchell felt real fear. She was out of her depth here. Collins would know how to handle the caller; she would be trained for this sort of thing. It was too late for that now, though; she had committed herself and needed to carry on the best way she could.

The laughter subsided and the voice of the caller came back on.

'Listen to me, Kate; you're the one who needs help and I'm going to give it to you. Go to this address and you will find out what happens when people insult me like you have.'

Mitchell scribbled down the address on her notepad.

'What you find there is your responsibility, Kate. Remember that, next time you write about me. Goodbye, for now.'

There was a short burst of hysterical laughter before the line went dead.

Chapter Seventeen

Collins had received a frantic call from Mitchell an hour earlier. She had called for Paul, her driver, and was on the way to the address that Mitchell had given her within ten minutes. On the way, she had made a number of calls to various colleagues, and expected all the necessary people to be at the scene in double quick time. She didn't know what they were going to find when they got there, but Mitchell had been so convinced by her caller that Collins had gone with her instincts and ordered a full mobilisation of her task force, including forensics and photographers.

As they arrived at the end of the side road off the A34 near Congleton, she was glad to see that the lane leading from the road had been cordoned off by the local police. There was a marked police car, with two uniformed officers and a detective, waiting for her party to arrive. She had issued strict orders that nobody should proceed any further until she arrived. She introduced herself to the detective in charge, leaving the uniformed officers to direct the rest of her team to the crime scene, and to keep any curious bypassers away.

The three of them drove along the track until they came to an old wooden farm gate which was partly open. It was obvious that the gate hadn't been used until recently by the length of the grass and brambles that twined around the rails. The snapped brambles and torn grass showed that someone had forced the gate open. They could see where someone had walked from the gate towards the old farmhouse, which was just visible through a screen of mature conifers.

Collins led the two detectives through the trees. She saw the derelict barn with much of its roof missing and turned towards it, all the time keeping one eye on the ground in case they disturbed any evidence that might be lying around. They picked their way through the long grass, careful to avoid stepping in the same tracks as the previous visitor had made. As they approached the building Collins could see through the partly-missing walls. She thought she caught a glimpse of something white; it struck her as out of place among all the greens and browns of the timbers and the foliage.

The door had rotted and fallen to the ground, leaving just the hinges still attached to the frame. Collins stopped cold as she came into the doorway, a sick feeling creeping down to her stomach. In front of her was the scene she had hoped she wouldn't find. The flash of white she had spotted through the walls was a discarded garment, probably a tee-shirt or top. There, right in the centre of the old barn, was the decapitated body of another female, the torso naked from the waist up and covered in blood. The arms were lifted and spread outwards; Collins could see the blue nylon rope that was tied around the victims' wrists, strung over the roof beams, holding the victim in an obscene, crucifix-like pose.

She made her way carefully towards the body; she could see the injuries were the same as the other victims. There was a gaping hole where the heart had been ripped from the body; the head had been hacked off, leaving numerous pieces of tissue hanging from the neck area. The detective behind her turned away, rushing a few yards towards the door before he vomited. Collins could sympathise with him; the first time she had seen one of these killings she had felt the same way.

Collins walked around the victim's body, looking closely for anything different from the other murder scenes. She noticed that the tee-shirt, like in the previous murders, had been ripped or cut; there seemed to be a piece missing. She saw it lying a few yards away in the longer grass. It had been determined by the forensic team that the strips of clothing which had been ripped from the main garments had been used as gags. She scribbled away in her notebook, recording everything she saw. She was looking for something different, a change of pattern or method. Collins jumped at the sound of her phone ringing; she looked at the display. It was Mitchell.

'Hello Kate,' she said. 'I'm afraid your information was correct. We have another victim down here.'

'Your men won't let me through, Andrea,' was the reply.

Damn, thought Collins; some people just wouldn't take orders. She had told Mitchell not to come to the crime scene. Maybe she won't be so keen if I let her see the body, she thought.

'Put the officer on the phone, Kate,' she said.

She instructed the officer to let Mitchell through the cordon and waited for her to arrive. Something fluttered in the breeze; it was a small piece of paper. She dashed after it, catching it before the wind took it away from the building. There was print on one side. It was a newspaper cutting. She turned it over and was shocked to see a picture of Kate Mitchell. This must have come from the article she had written, Collins mused; and the killer must have brought it here. It was a worrying development. The killer had first called Mitchell, and now had cut a picture of her from the paper. She wondered if this was important. She must speak to Davies about this; she didn't want to put Mitchell in any danger.

Chapter Eighteen

James was on the couch in Davies's consulting room. He was agitated; he was in a deep trance, and had been recounting his dream from the night before. Davies had tried leading him through the dream slowly; he wanted to cajole James into revealing the identity of the person in his dreams, or at least determine whether James actually knew whose eyes he was looking through.

Davies was struggling to keep James coherent. His thoughts were drifting, his story jumping randomly from one event to another. It was becoming harder to understand his ramblings. Davies made sure his recorder was on and functioning properly. It could be useful to listen to the interview later. He might pick up on something he had missed during the session.

It wasn't going as well as Davies had expected. Normally when he had a patient under hypnosis it was quite easy to regress them, taking them back to their early years. In his experience that was the place where the roots of most of the problems would be found. In James's case there seemed to be a block; he could get no further back than the beginning of the nightmares.

But this was an unusual case; he already suspected that the dreams that James was having weren't connected to a trauma suffered in his childhood, but the result of some sort of psychic link he shared with the killer. The functions of most of the human brain were still not understood by science, but Davies knew recent studies had shown that people could communicate with each other without speech because they were on the same radio frequency. All neuroscientists had accepted that the brain emits electrical pulses or radio waves; where Davies, and many others of his profession, differed from the mainstream was in the belief that, while each brain is unique, in extremely rare circumstances two brains could share the same characteristics and the same frequency. Therefore, he believed, it was quite feasible that two people, totally unconnected with each other in normal everyday life, could share thoughts and even experiences with each other, without ever having met. They wouldn't be aware of what they were experiencing; they would just write them off as strange dreams, a feeling of having done something or been somewhere, but knowing they had never been to the place in question, or done the things they were dreaming of.

Davies had seen this phenomenon with his own eyes, and believed firmly that it was a fact of science. He was becoming even more certain that here was just such a case; the difference being that here, the person James was subconsciously communicating with was a mass murderer. Davies wondered if the killer was aware of James. Was it a two way connection; did the killer, in turn, see through James's eyes? There were more questions than answers here and Davies needed to change that. He would have to ask James about his wife. He had never mentioned her in his trances; he knew they had been married for about five years and that the dreams had started at about the time they had been married. They would obviously be close, sometimes a common factor in psychic communications. The killer was a woman. Too many coincidences, thought Davies.

James was still rambling incoherently; Davies tried to follow his mutterings. He was talking about a barn; someone called Julie was mentioned. He didn't recall seeing that name in the case files. He would have to speak to Collins about that. There were new details this session; James described a bar or club, Davies couldn't tell which. He also talked in stilted sentences of a trapdoor and a cellar.

Davies tried to calm James down. It sounded like he may be describing the lair of the killer. In a typical case, they usually had a hideaway somewhere. Though this wasn't exactly a typical case, if only he could get more information he might be able to pinpoint the place. He couldn't use anything of a personal nature that James told him, but if he found out the location, that would satisfy his conscience. He would only be passing on an address; he wouldn't be betraying James, and he would be doing his duty as a doctor, as well as his duty as a member of the investigation team. He was clearly going to get no further today and so decided to wake James from his trance.

James woke slowly and started to relax, his tension seeming to visibly disappear as Davies studied him.

'Welcome back, James; how are you feeling? Could you manage a few more questions?'

'Hello, Doc; yes, I suppose I could if it will help with these damn nightmares,' replied James.

'How do you get along with your wife these days, James? Are things okay between you?'

'What has my wife got to do with this?' said James rather sharply; Davies noted the rise in tension.

'Just answer the questions please, James. We both want to resolve your problem and to do that I need to ask a great many questions, so please be patient, and have a little faith. I have done this before, you know, James.'

'Sorry Doctor. Fire away; what do you want to know?'

'Have you discussed your dreams with your wife?'

'Not yet; I don't like to bother her. To be quite honest, we hardly talk at all. We seem to miss each other most of the time, and if she isn't asleep then I usually am. I think too much work takes its toll on both of us.'

'Yes, it can be disruptive to a good relationship. James, your wife; sorry, I don't recall her name, does she have any problems sleeping that you know about? Does she have any dreams or restlessness?'

James suddenly had a flashback to that place, the one where he had seen the eyes on the vase; he heard the voice again, and the sinister whisper, 'Amy.' His flesh crawled; he hadn't recalled that before while he was fully conscious.

'Not that I know of, Doctor. Amy sleeps like a log.'

The words were out of his mouth before he knew he had said them; he hesitated, confused.

Davies noticed the hesitation, and also that James's wife wasn't called Jayne.

'Are you alright, James? Do you need a break?'

'No, no. I'm fine thanks, Doc. Just a small flashback.'

'Do you have many of these flashbacks when you're conscious, James?'

'Not usually Doc; they do seem to be getting more regular though.'

'I want you to record them all for me, if you can. Keep a diary of the times and content of each flashback. Anything you may recognise in your dreams could be very helpful.'

'I will, Doc; they only come briefly though and there's not usually much in them.'

'That doesn't matter, James; any small piece of information may be some help with your problem. Now, one last question. Does anyone ever speak in your dreams, to you or to a third party, and have you ever heard any names?'

Davies knew from his probing while James was under hypnosis that he had heard voices in his dreams, though he hadn't been able to articulate what he had heard. Possibly he could remember more now he was awake. James answered, once again, seemingly involuntarily:

'No, Doc. I hear voices, people talking, but I can't make sense of them.'

James was shocked at himself again; he had clearly heard the voice whisper Amy. Why had he said that, he wondered? Why did he feel a need to protect Amy? Davies was a good reader of people and he could tell that James wasn't being as forthcoming with his answers as he could be. He needed to find out why. What was James hiding; was he trying to protect someone? He had noticed the way that James had answered certain questions almost automatically, as if from a script; he guessed that James didn't know himself why he wasn't being altogether truthful. The look of confusion on his face suggested that to Davies.

The phone on Davies's desk rang. He had instructed his secretary not to disturb him; it must be important, he thought as he picked it up.

'Excuse me, James,' he said.

'Doctor, there's a call from Detective Collins, she says it's urgent.'

'Put her through please, Sarah,' Davies said to his secretary.

'Good morning Detective Collins, how can I help you?' asked Davies. He listened for a few seconds as Collins explained about the new victim.

'I can be at the scene in twenty minutes, Detective. I will leave straight away.' He replaced the receiver and looked sympathetically at his despondent patient.

'I'm sorry James, but some unavoidable business has come up. I must finish for today. Please come in to the office to see me in the morning.'

'Of course,' said James dejectedly, managing a weak smile as he left the room. The poor man, thought Davies.

Chapter Nineteen

Mitchell arrived at the barn ten minutes after calling Collins.

'Good morning, Kate,' Collins greeted her, 'I hope you haven't had breakfast.'

'That bad?' asked Mitchell.

'I'm afraid so, Kate. It's not a pretty picture. Do you want to see?'

'Yes I do, it will give me a feel for the story,' said Mitchell.

Collins felt her anger flare. The bloody story was all that mattered; what about that poor girl, hanging like a piece of discarded meat from the beams of the barn? She took a deep breath; Mitchell was just being professional after all. Still, it would give her a little satisfaction when Mitchell saw the body. Nobody could see that sort of sight without feeling sickened to the stomach.

Collins led Mitchell round to the entrance and stopped in the opening to let Mitchell take in the scene. She saw her face visibly whiten; good, she thought, maybe she might learn a lesson today.

'Follow me, Kate, exactly in my tracks; we don't want to disturb any evidence.'

Mitchell followed Collins until they reached the body.

'Dear God, how could anyone do this Andrea?' she gasped.

She could feel herself trembling as she surveyed the scene of carnage before her. She was using her professional eye to take in the scene, while at the same time her mind was reeling at the monstrous nature of the crime.

'That's why we are here, Kate; to find out who did this, and why.'

Mitchell was looking decidedly nauseous, thought Collins. Well, if she wanted to play in the big league, she would have to take the lows as well as the highs.

'Tell me about your phone call, Kate. I want every detail, however small.'

Mitchell got her notebook out; like any good journalist, she had recorded every word, every detail, including the laughter she had heard from the caller. She recounted her conversation, leaving nothing out.

'I'm sorry I couldn't get a recording or call you straight away, Andrea; I was taken completely by surprise. It's not every day that you receive a call from a lunatic.'

'Oh, I get them nearly everyday, Kate. We have to call them chief constables or commissioners,' quipped Collins. She wanted to relax Mitchell if she could.

Mitchell managed a half smile; it wasn't a smiling sort of place. She looked with fresh eyes at Collins; how could she be so blasé about this? Maybe it was her way of dealing with the horror of it all. She wondered if she herself could cope with the line of work Collins was in, seeing this sort of thing day in day out; how could she still sleep at night? Collins interrupted her reverie.

'We've found something here that concerns me, Kate; it's worrying, and it concerns you.'

Mitchell looked at Collins.

'What do you mean it concerns me?'

Collins reached into her coat pocket, retrieving the evidence bag that she had placed there. She held the bag out to Mitchell. As she handed it to Mitchell she watched her face closely. First she looked at the printed side with a slightly puzzled look on her face, and then she turned it over and saw her own picture staring at her from the newspaper cutting. It didn't register at first; Collins watched Mitchell's face change as it slowly dawned on her what she was looking at. Her mouth gaped open as she realised the significance of the picture. The thing that disturbed Collins most was the word BITCH, written in red across the bottom of the picture.

'What does this mean; where did you find it?' blurted Mitchell, clearly rattled.

'We don't know yet; Dr. Davies is on his way over here right now,' said Collins.

'But why is my picture here?' insisted Mitchell.

'It was left here, Kate, I assume by the killer; it would appear that your article has upset her.'

Collins' phone rang; it was the officer at the barrier. 'Dr. Davies is here, along with the forensic people,' he said.

'Thank you, send them up please,' said Collins.

She left Mitchell staring at the body and walked down the path to greet Davies and her forensic people. She gave orders to the technicians and, as they made their way to the barn, she explained to Davies the circumstances of the latest murder.

They walked through the screen of trees and Davies felt his heart miss a beat when he saw the ruins of the old barn. James had mentioned a barn that very morning.

'Do we have a name for the victim, Andrea?' he asked Collins.

'Not yet Doctor, the forensic search may come up with something if we're lucky.'

This was the first time Davies had attended a murder scene. He was appalled at the sight but he was an old time professional; he had worked on cases like this before and he knew how depraved people could be. He looked around. The sky was clear; it was a beautiful day, birds singing, the smells and sounds of the countryside all around them. But amidst all that beauty, someone inherently evil had created a vision of hell, a vision he didn't want to cast his eyes on again. He must help Collins find this killer before she struck again.

'We did find this, though,' said Collins, handing over the picture to Davies; he studied it, recognising it from the article that had been leaked to the press, he assumed by Collins, in view of the fact that Kate Mitchell was standing a few yards away from him, watching the forensic people go about their grisly task.

'Here at the scene?' asked Davies.

'Yes, right by the body, it was blowing around the barn,' replied Collins.

'Have your people tested it yet, Andrea?'

'Not yet, I can get them to look at it right now though, if you think it's important.'

'Please do, Andrea; ask them to check the substance of the writing on the picture.' He removed his glasses and wiped the lenses on his handkerchief.

'It appears you may have angered the killer, Andrea; or, more to the point, Miss Mitchell appears to have angered her.'

'We were trying to provoke a response from her,' said Collins.

'Well, it certainly looks as if you have got your wish, Andrea,' said Davies harshly.

'We had to do something; we haven't had so much as a single lead. We can't just wait until she makes a mistake. You said yourself, she might never make one.' Collins was being defensive now and Davies could see why.

'It's okay Andrea; I'm not saying you shouldn't have done it, just that you should have consulted me first. I would have told you what to say in the article. You can sometimes push so hard that you tip them over the edge. At the moment our killer is probably working to some sort of pattern or agenda, even she might not know what that pattern is but there invariably is one. If we push too hard she might lose all sense of reality and start killing more prolifically.'

'Point taken, Doctor; next time I make sure I speak to you first.'

There was a shout from a technician.

'Detective, we have something here.'

Collins, Mitchell, and Davies all went over to where the technicians had set up their mobile lab.

'First of all, the writing on the picture is written in blood, the victim's blood, one hundred percent positive match;

secondly, we found a purse in the long grass. Fingerprints on the purse confirm it as the victim's. There were no prints on the cutting.'

'Thanks, John,' Collins said. 'Was there any identification?'

'Yes. We have a driver's licence and a gym membership card, both in the name of Julie Wilson, aged twenty five. Her address is in Congleton.'

Davies felt his heart skip again; James had mentioned a Julie in his trance that morning. He had also mentioned a barn; now he was here in that very barn, with a sadly deceased Julie. Davies looked down at the picture of the dead girl, a snapshot taken for her gym membership card; such a pretty girl, he thought, such a tragic waste of life. This was fast becoming a personal nightmare; he was torn between his Hippocratic Oath and his duty to his colleagues and the victims.

There was nothing else they could do here; Collins suggested that she, Mitchell and Davies should find somewhere to have coffee and discuss the day's developments. They drove the few miles to Congleton, where they found a quiet café and ordered drinks. Collins didn't want to go too far away from Congleton; she would have interviews to carry out later in the day, with any family or friends of the dead girl they may find. She called her driver and told him to reserve rooms at the nearest motel; it would be a long and stressful day, perhaps even night.

Chapter Twenty

James had gone home early again; his headaches seemed to be getting both more severe and more regular. His mind had been playing over the interview he had with Davies that morning. Davies had asked him about Amy, but for some reason he hadn't been altogether truthful. He wasn't intending to mislead Davies; something just told him not to mention everything he saw in his dreams. Maybe he was worried they might think him mad, and lock him up in some mental institution.

He arrived home and made himself a cold drink; he would sit for a while until his head cleared, then he would go to talk to Amy about his dreams. Talking was a therapy in itself, they said; he picked up the newspaper from the sideboard. He hadn't read it when he bought it home. There was an article on the front page about a serial killer. He scanned quickly through the article, wondering what sort of sick person could carry out such awful crimes. Those people should definitely be hung, he thought.

There was a small square cut from the paper, just below the headline, next to where the journalist's credit was printed. That was odd; Amy didn't usually take much notice of the newspapers. He read through the story again. There was a Detective Collins heading the investigation, it said. James wondered if it was the same Collins who had been in contact with Dr. Davies at work. James knew that Davies did work for the police. What a strange coincidence, he thought.

He remembered Collins from when she had visited the lab recently. She had been very polite, and although she was a little old for James she was still a striking looking woman. There wasn't much detail in the article, just basic background; James didn't for one minute associate the story with his dreams. As far as he was aware, dreams were just dreams.

James went up to the bedroom; Amy was already in bed as usual. He sat on the edge of the bed and whispered to her.

'Are you asleep, Amy?'

'I was until you woke me up,' she snapped.

'I'm sorry, but I need to talk to you. Amy, I haven't been sleeping well, for a long time now. I've been having these nightmares. I've been seeing things ... terrible things. It's gotten so bad ... I went to see a psychiatrist,' he blurted out.

There was silence, and then in a cold voice Amy said:

'And what did your psychiatrist tell you, James?'

'Nothing really, he just asks a lot of questions. He's been giving me hypnosis to try and explore my subconscious mind. He says the problem will probably be from a bad experience when I was a child.'

'Why don't you try sleeping tablets? There's some in the medicine cabinet. I'm getting tired of your nightmares as well, James. You keep me awake nearly every night.'

James was shocked; Amy knew about his nightmares and had never mentioned them. Why had she never asked about them?

'Why didn't you tell me that you knew I was having bad dreams?'

'Because we never see each other James, I can't talk in my sleep.'

'Thank you for your concern Amy, its nice to know you care,' James said acidly. He softened his tone.

'Look Amy, I think it would do us both some good to get away for a few days, what do you think? Shall we pack up and have a long weekend away?'

'If that's what you want then fine, just let me know when we're going. I need to get some sleep now, I'm worn out. Goodnight.'

James went back downstairs. He rooted out his address book; there was a number for a nice hotel just outside Nottingham, where he had stayed overnight for a conference a few months back. It was classy and had easy access to the countryside around those parts; there was nothing like a few days in the open air to clear your head he thought. He phoned the reception and reserved a room for four nights, starting the next day. They would understand at work; he was sure they wouldn't give him any problems for having unauthorised leave.

He went back upstairs, taking care not to disturb Amy again. She was in a foul mood, and he could do without arguments. When Amy was in that mood you would get more sense if you talked to yourself. He showered and shaved before drying himself off, and crawling exhausted into bed.

Chapter Twenty One

Collins had been back at the motel for half an hour, carrying out a gruelling series of interviews with friends and family of the latest victim. Like many of the others she had a problem; hers was drugs, her family had said, mainly soft stuff, but the family didn't approve of any sort of drugs unless they were prescribed.

The friends had been helpful. Collins had obtained a good description of the killer, who had been spotted going to the washroom with the victim. After that no-one had seen her alive. The description matched that of the witnesses from the previous killing.

She had also interviewed the manager of the establishment where the abduction took place. He had reported seeing that the fire door to the rear of the building had been opened. When he went to investigate, he saw a dark coloured Ford saloon pulling out of the back street; and he noted it was a Manchester number plate. But after checking the premises were secure he decided not to take any further action. If only he had been there a couple of minutes earlier thought Collins, he might have prevented the killing.

Mitchell had also checked into the motel. She was now taking notes down for Collins, who was clearly too tired to do them herself. She had showered and was now lounging back in her armchair with her feet up and a glass of wine in her hand.

'Davies seemed like a good sort Andrea; has he got much experience in this sort of case?'

'He's recognised as the leading authority on the subject. He worked with the Americans on a number of cases; you should read the profile he made up for me. It's very interesting reading.'

Mitchell coughed, slightly uncomfortably.

'I took the liberty of reading it when you were in the shower' she said apologetically. Andrea just laughed.

'You're a nosey cow Kate, that nose of yours will get chopped off one of these days if you're not careful.'

'I know, but I just can't help myself,' replied Mitchell with a smile.

'Don't worry Kate, I do it all the time. I'm always rooting around peoples desks, reading their files.'

They both laughed at that; they needed a little light relief after the day they had just endured.

'Andrea, I really am worried about this picture. I know Davies said it's unlikely that she would deviate from her pattern, but it still worries me. There's always a first time for everything.'

'Don't worry about security Kate, I'll have a patrol car make regular visits to your apartment. Just keep yourself in busy areas when you go out, and report anything you find suspicious to me personally, at any time, day or night.'

'Thanks Andrea. I will feel more secure if I know some of your people are keeping an eye out for me.'

'We need to go over every file again from start to finish. There is a pattern in there somewhere and we need to find it. Davies thinks that if we find the pattern we find the killer,' Collins mused.

'We must be missing something,' Mitchell said. Collins noted the 'we'; well, it wouldn't do any harm for Kate to feel part of her team, and she would ensure total cooperation that way.

The car enquiries had drawn a blank; as with every other lead that they had it seemed to fizzle out after the initial excitement. It must be very frustrating thought Mitchell, to work on cases like this all the time, knowing that the only realistic chance of solving the crimes rested with the perpetrator making a mistake; or perhaps with a member of the public, who, by pure chance, would stumble across a vital piece of evidence and report it to the police, probably not even knowing how important their find was.

'Tomorrow we'll go to the Task Force incident room,' said Collins; she had decided to go back to the beginning. Maybe with Kate looking at the files, she could get a different perspective on the case. Kate was sharp, and she might just spot something that she and the team had been missing.

'I want you to go over all the files with me. We have a lot of photographic evidence, and I warn you that it isn't a pretty sight Kate.'

'After what I saw this morning I think I can handle anything,' said Mitchell.

Collins looked over at Mitchell. She certainly was a tough lady she thought; she would make a good detective. Maybe she could convert her after this case was over; but probably not. She would find most of the day to day police work too mundane. She seemed like the type who would easily become bored.

'I believe you can,' she said. 'Well, I won't detain you any longer Kate, I need to get my beauty sleep again. I don't seem to be getting much lately, and I'll thank you for not making any sarcastic comments if you don't mind. Good night.'

Mitchell smiled. They were very much on the same wavelength. It was good to have someone like Andrea to work with. She would make a good journalist she thought as she watched Collins leave to go to her own room; but for now, she could do with some sleep herself.

Chapter Twenty Two

Collins arrived at the Task Force HQ early to prepare for a busy day of meetings with members of her team and other interested parties. She chaired the briefing with her whole team at nine o'clock, and they went over all the latest developments in the case. There still wasn't much to go on; they were looking for a woman, the victims were picked because they appeared in most cases to be the most vulnerable. That suggested that the killer was stalking them, trying to identify a suitable target, before abducting them and performing her ritual on them. It was a ritual, Davies had said, a pattern of behaviour; Collins was frustrated because she could see no motive but Davies had told her again that motives were almost impossible to find in cases like these. She could hear him in her mind, coolly explaining himself like a teacher; 'The serial killer's mind works totally different from that of a normal person. There is no rational explanation for their behaviour, but there will be a reason. In the killer's mind, everything she does will be for a purpose. She is working towards a goal; one which, in her mind, is perfectly rational.'

Kate Mitchell arrived at the office at ten thirty as instructed; she was pale and nervous-looking.

'Good morning Kate,' said Collins, 'are you feeling alright? You look a little pale.'

'Morning, Andrea. I'm fine thanks, apart from this.'

She rooted in her bag and came out with an envelope which she handed to Collins.

'This was in my mail tray this morning; hand delivered to the reception, and no one saw who delivered it.'

Collins turned it over in her hands. 'Is it from the killer?' she asked.

'I think so, yes. I'm no expert, but it looks pretty damn authentic to me.'

Collins opened the envelope and took out the single sheet of paper; on it was a typed message to Mitchell.

'ARE YOU SATSFIED NOW BITCH, MAYBE YOU WILL REMEMBER THAT GIRLS FACE THE NEXT TIME YOU DEFAME MY CHARACTER IN THAT FILTHY RAG YOU CALL A NEWSPAPER. YOUR RESPONSIBILITY KATE. HAVE YOU GOT NO HEART?'

Collins placed the letter carefully on her desk.

'Forensics will have to look over it,' she said to Mitchell, 'though I doubt if they will find anything. This one is very clever. All we have found is a single hair at the scene of a crime, and that was a dead hair, probably from a wig.'

Collins looked at Mitchell; she was trembling slightly.

'She was obviously upset by what you wrote about her. I'll increase the presence on your apartment and give you a minder until this is resolved.'

'Thanks, Andrea. It's getting a bit worrying for me now. Do you think she might come after me?'

Collins was worried too. The letter was mocking them; the reference to having no heart was a clear indication of that. It was also clear that the killer was very angry with Kate and wanted to punish her. Collins hoped that punishment would be limited to the killer trying to play on any guilt that Kate may feel, but she wasn't sure; in fact she wasn't sure of anything right at this moment.

Davies had now arrived and after exchanging greetings with the remaining team members, along with Collins and Mitchell, he was shown the letter.

'This is very serious, Andrea; your provocation has clearly worked. The only problem is, what will she do now? If she changes her pattern we may well get a break in the case, but it could also lead to her becoming more active if she is agitated. There's just no telling, we can only react to her actions.'

'Surely there is something you can do,' said Mitchell. 'Somebody must know her, work with her or live with her.'

'That is quite possible Kate; unfortunately our killer may be a perfectly normal person outwardly. She is probably not even aware of what she is doing herself.'

'But how could she not know? She must get blood on her; doesn't she wake up and wonder where it came from?'

'She could have multiple personalities; the one that is killing will be very clever. She will go to any extremes to cover her tracks, cleaning her clothes when she arrives home and making sure that when her other personality emerges, she won't have any inkling of what she has done.'

'Well how the hell are we meant to stop her killing then?' said Mitchell angrily.

'We need to find a pattern. Perhaps the timing of the killings, or the places she kills; somewhere there will be a routine for her, we just have to find it.'

'And if we don't find a pattern?' said Mitchell.

'Then we have to hope that she makes some sort of mistake. That's the way these monsters are usually caught I'm afraid; one day she will make a small mistake and we will have her.' Davies sounded more confident than he felt.

'Don't you have a list of people with these disorders, Andrea? Surely she must have been treated for it at some time.'

'It just doesn't work that way Kate,' said Collins. 'You read the profile that Dr. Davies did for us, Kate. Lets not get worked up about this thing; cool heads are what are needed here.'

'I know. I'm sorry Andrea, it's just a shade frightening when you receive personal hate mail from a serial killer.'

'I suggest that if we are to make progress we should be searching for the pattern,' said Davies. 'Andrea and I have both studied every piece of material available; why don't you see if you can give us a fresh view of things, Kate?'

'Give me a few hours to sift through all of this and lets see where it might lead,' said Mitchell as she opened the first file and started to read.

Davies had another appointment to keep and had to leave; he also had a consultation with James Elliot that afternoon, and he was really going to have to push him hard. Things were getting out of hand; he needed answers now.

Chapter Twenty Three

James had phoned the lab first thing in the morning and spoken to his boss. He knew he was having problems, and he readily agreed that James should take a few days off; it would do him good, he had said. He left a message with Davies's secretary to let Davies know he was out of town for a few days. They were taking Amy's car; she insisted it was more comfortable and had more room than his. He couldn't see what difference it made, but he didn't want an argument and so they had left home before lunch and arrived at the hotel in the early afternoon.

They registered at the reception and were shown to their room; it was very plush, deep pile carpets and amazingly comfortable furniture. I could get used to this James thought, as he looked from his balcony over miles of open countryside. It was a bright, cloudless day; James decided he would go for a walk and take advantage of the fine weather while it lasted. Amy was asleep already.

James wasn't going to disturb her and risk an argument, so he left quietly on his own, following a path that led him through the nearby woods and down to a small river. The river meandered down through the valley in front of him, the water swirling and racing along, carrying all sorts of natural flotsam with it. He wandered along, following the river bank, taking in the sights and the fresh smell of the countryside; by the time he turned round to make the return journey he felt refreshed, his mind clear for the first time in weeks. It was amazing the effect a change of scenery could have on a person he thought. He made his way leisurely, taking a short cut across a meadow where a few families had settled to enjoy picnics, basking in the warm glow of the sun.

The long walk had tired him by the time he arrived back at the hotel, so he decided to have an afternoon nap. He would be awake by tea time and could sit out on the terrace and enjoy his meal as he watched the sun go down over the valley. He went up to his room; no sooner had his head touched the pillow than he was asleep.

Amy had been disturbed when James settled onto the bed; she rose quietly and went to the bathroom where she showered and dressed. She needed to go into town. Nottingham wasn't part of her plans; this visit was an unexpected bonus, and she would take advantage of the visit. If she could find a suitable collection piece while she was in the city, she would collect it tonight, or tomorrow maybe; she had bought an ice box with her so she could keep her pieces fresh. It wouldn't do to have them start smelling before the presentation.

Amy had heard about Nottingham; it was a lively city and they said that there were six females to every male. She didn't know how true that was, but as she walked around the city centre, it certainly seemed to be. Everywhere she looked was crowded with groups of females. Perfect, she thought with a satisfied smile; this should be an easy night. She tried a few bars but was disappointed with the quality she saw; she was a perfectionist, and only the very best would do.

It was four thirty; some of the shops were getting ready to close for the day, and she needed a dress for tonight. She had to find somewhere quickly; she had torn her other dress last time she went out collecting. She spotted a charity shop a few doors away. She had bought excellent quality clothes from those shops before, at a fraction of their true value. She rushed to make it to the shop and was relieved to see that it didn't close until five thirty.

Amy always tried to wear a nice little black number when she was out collecting. Not only was it her favourite colour, it was also the one which suited her most, bringing the best out of her looks. The most important reason she chose black though was that if she was stopped by the police while driving, they wouldn't be able to see any blood stains on her clothing.

She found the dress racks and started looking through them. There were quite a few black dresses, and she wanted to make sure she had the best. She jumped as a voice said over her shoulder:

'Good afternoon! Can I be of any assistance?'

It was a woman's voice, sultry and friendly sounding; she turned to face the voice, answering as she did so.

'Yes please, I need help picking one of these dresses. Maybe you could help me choose?'

'Certainly, I'd be glad to,' came the reply, delivered with a smile that made Amy's heart skip a beat. She was looking into the most stunning pair of ice blue eyes that she had ever seen; she had to catch her breath. This girl was perfect. Amy was having trouble focusing on what she was there for; she managed to drag her stare away from the girl's eyes.

'Thanks. If I hold them up, can you just tell me which one you think suits me best?'

'Sure,' said Michelle; she was wearing a badge which stated her name and position as shop manager.

They picked the same dress as each other and laughed about having good taste. Amy was impressed; not only was Michelle stunning in looks, she also had one of those infectious personalities that always seemed to put people at ease. Mother will absolutely adore this one thought Amy; she had already decided that Michelle would take pride of place in her collection. It was such a shame. She would love to keep this one for herself.

Amy paid with cash.

'Thanks for your help Michelle,' she said, pointedly looking at the name badge that the girl wore. 'It's so nice to get service with a smile these days, especially one as beautiful as yours.'

Michelle was slightly embarrassed but flattered at the same time; it was always nice to get a compliment, and this girl seemed quite open and genuine.

'Thank you,' she said, unable to contain another beaming smile. 'You're making me blush now.'

Amy laughed. Such innocence, she thought; but that would change soon enough, when she had her tied up and stripped waiting for the ritual to begin. Amy could barely keep her excitement under control. She had to make a conscious effort to look relaxed and normal, and so she said her goodbyes and left the shop.

There was a bar just a few doors down the street and on the opposite side from the shop which Michelle worked at. Amy went into the bar and ordered coffee before taking a window seat that overlooked the front of the charity shop. Ten minutes and the shop would be closed. She decided to follow Michelle to see where she went; she might have to engineer a 'chance' meeting, if she could find out where Michelle lived or socialised.

At five minutes after closing time Michelle emerged from the shop door, keys in hand, and turned to lock up for the day. As she was locking the door an older woman stopped and spoke to her; they obviously knew each other from their demeanour. They walked along the street, past Amy's bar and towards the car park at the rear of the shops. Amy left the bar in as casual manner as she could manage and hurried along after the two women.

It seemed that Amy's luck was in today; they were standing by a small, three-door car, chatting away without a care in the world. The older woman was searching in her handbag; probably for her car keys, Amy guessed correctly.

Amy had parked her vehicle on the next car park, and was in her car with the engine running within two minutes. The other two women had just got into their car, and were now driving slowly around to the exit. Amy waited until the car had cleared the exit before making her own way out into the traffic flow. It was reasonably quiet on the road, so she shouldn't have any trouble following them.

Amy didn't know the roads here so she had to concentrate; she kept them in sight as they drove out of the city and into a more rural setting. They drove for about fifteen miles, before coming to a halt in what appeared to be a large village. She counted three pubs and a hotel; the two women pulled into the third and last pub car park. Amy stopped a few hundred yards down the road, and watched the two of them disappear through the door of the pub before driving straight to the hotel and booking a room for the night. She needed to shower, and change into her black dress. She would have to take a chance that Michelle would still be in the pub when she arrived.

Amy wasn't disappointed. She saw Michelle straight away; she could hardly miss her. Michelle was on the stage belting out a ballad on the karaoke machine, and she had a fantastic voice. Amy was transfixed; she couldn't take her eyes off Michelle as she hit the high notes at the end of the song. She tore her gaze away from the stage, searching for the other woman who had arrived with Michelle, and spotted her towards the back of the pub, sitting alone. Good; they had no men with them.

Amy bought herself a drink from the bar, and made her way casually to the table next to Michelle's friend. She applauded enthusiastically when Michelle finished another song, which drew approving looks from Michelle's friend. The audience shouted for an encore and Michelle, obviously enjoying herself, obliged them, belting out another great hit in that incredible voice.

'She's very good, isn't she?' Amy said to the woman on the next table.

'She is,' said the woman. 'She's been doing that for years.'

'You know it's strange,' said Amy, 'but I'm sure that's the girl who sold me a dress today in Nottingham centre. What a coincidence! I'm staying at the hotel over the road while I'm here on business.'

The other woman laughed. 'You must be the one who bought the little black number then. You made her day; she never stopped talking about it all the way home. She does like her compliments, you know.'

Amy laughed and carried on chatting to the woman, whose name, she discovered, was Moira; they were getting along like old friends. Amy's charm was working again, she saw with satisfaction. Michelle had finished singing and was making her way back to where Amy sat with Moira, taking in the compliments from the rest of the pub customers with a beaming smile on her face.

Michelle arrived at the table, a look of surprise on her face.

'Hello again,' she said to Amy. 'Your dress looks great on.'

Amy flashed her most dazzling smile. 'You remember me then, Michelle. Thank you; it was you who picked it for me.'

Michelle took her seat alongside them and sipped at her drink.

'So you came all this way for the karaoke?' she giggled.

'Oh no,' Amy laughed, 'I'm here on business. I'm staying at the local hotel; a friend recommended it to me.'

The three of them all chatted away, and were getting on well. Amy was delighted; things were going just as she had planned. She had parked her car at the back of the pub, only a few feet from the fire escape, her belongings all in the boot; she had come here well prepared.

Amy was stretching the limits of her own patience; she was struggling to suppress her urge to get Michelle on her own, into a position where she could slip the sedative into her drink. She would have to use a shorter measure than usual; she couldn't have Michelle passing out before she was ready. She would give her enough to make her feel drowsy, and then suggest a trip to the bathroom to wash her face and freshen up.

Although outwardly happy and relaxed, Michelle was feeling slightly uncomfortable. She didn't know why; maybe it was intuition, she thought. She found it a little strange that this woman Jayne should remember her and use her name in such a familiar way as soon as they had met again. She didn't believe in coincidences; she was watching Jayne closely, trying to figure out if she was genuine or if this hadn't been a chance meeting after all. She could tell that Jayne found her attractive. That didn't worry her in itself; she wasn't interested in that sort of relationship. But if Jayne had followed her here, then that was unusual behaviour to say the least. If she had wanted to make a pass at her, she could have easily done it without going to all this trouble. Michelle wondered if she was being paranoid as she watched Jayne chatting to Moira.

She'd had the unpleasant experience of having a stalker a few years before, an ex who'd become obsessed with her. She had called the police then when it had become so bad that she couldn't leave her house without being followed by the weirdo. Ever since that incident she had been sensitive to people paying her too much attention. She would be safe in here though, where she knew most of the customers. She laughed at herself; she was being paranoid again.

Amy was growing impatient. There hadn't been an opportunity to spike Michelle's drink yet, and time was moving swiftly towards the end of the night. Her chance came when Moira went to the bathroom while Michelle was at the bar buying some crisps. She quickly slipped the drug into Michelle's glass, made sure it had dissolved properly, then sat back and waited. It would only be a matter of time now before Michelle drank it and became drowsy.

Michelle kept glancing at the mirror behind the bar. As she saw Moira go to the bathroom, leaving Jayne alone at the table, she caught movement in the corner of her eye and looked hard at the mirror. She was sure that Jayne had leaned over the table and picked her glass up; but as she stared at the table, Jayne appeared to be relaxed as she watched the entertainment.

Michelle returned to the table. Moira was back, chatting happily away to Jayne. Michelle picked up her glass and studied it; she couldn't see anything amiss, and once again she admonished herself for being paranoid. She put the glass to her lips and took a sip; Jayne smiled at her. Why was she looking so smug she wondered, her paranoia creeping back.

She took another sip of her drink and was aware of a strange taste; it was like powder on her tongue. She had a keen sense of taste and knew there was something in her drink that shouldn't be there. She looked at Jayne across the table. She was smiling, that smug expression on her face again. Michelle wasn't afraid to speak her mind.

'You've put something in my drink Jayne, what are you playing at?'

Jayne was clearly taken aback.

'I don't know what you mean,' she said to Michelle.

Moira looked at each of them in turn; Jayne had a hurt expression on her face.

'Don't be fooled by that look Moira,' said Michelle, growing angry; 'I saw her put something in my drink while I was at the bar. Here, taste it,' she said, handing the glass to Moira.

Amy's face had become flushed; she was boiling over with rage.

'How dare you,' she said, trying to bluff her way out of the situation.

'No, how dare you!' said Michelle. 'I want to know what you put in my drink!'

Amy was in a corner; she had to get out of here quickly before this escalated into a serious incident.

'Right, that's it! I'm not staying here to be insulted,' she stormed, rising from the table and picking up her bag as if to leave. Michelle had the bit between her teeth now and she wouldn't let it go.

'You're going nowhere, not until you tell me what you put in my drink.'

She stood directly in front of Amy so that she couldn't pass her to reach the doors. Other people were watching now and Amy could barely contain her anger.

'Get out of my way, now!' she said to Michelle, raising her voice further.

Michelle didn't move; Amy finally snapped. She had visions of her quest coming to a premature end, and she would never find peace if that happened. Her hand shot out and slapped Michelle hard across the right cheek.

'Out of my way you bitch!' she screamed hysterically.

Michelle shook her head, her eyes watering from the blow, but she stood her ground as Jayne screamed at her again. Michelle had learnt the hard way that the only way to face aggression was to hit the aggressor back twice as hard; they didn't like their own medicine. She bunched her fist and with every ounce of strength she had she launched a swinging blow towards Jayne's face. She saw the shock as her fist connected, just below her eye. Jayne stumbled back, falling into the table; her face was throbbing, and she had to get out of this place quickly. The doors were barred by all the onlookers so she made a dash for the toilets, where she knew she could escape through the fire exit.

Michelle and some of the other customers went after her; she had questions to answer. As they entered the corridor which housed the toilet area, they were just in time to see Jayne kick open the crash bar on the fire door and make her escape through the exit.

They arrived at the door just as Jayne pulled out of the car park with a screech of tyres and a smell of burning rubber. One of the customers wrote down part of the car registration number. He had got the first four digits correct, as well as the make, model, and colour.

There was a great deal of excitement at the pub; it was a quiet village, and things like this never happened there. The landlord called the police who were soon on the way over, and some of the locals had gone to the hotel to see if the woman had returned there. Her room was empty; she had quite obviously never intended to stay in it. If that was the case, said the men, her aim must have been to abduct or harm Michelle.

The police duly arrived and started the long process of taking statements. It would take them all night to file their reports; they didn't realise the importance of what had happened there tonight. Only later would they realise that they could have prevented further murders; another opportunity had slipped away.

Chapter Twenty Four

News of the attempted abduction had been slow to reach the city police headquarters. The rural areas didn't get much attention and so it would be nearly twenty-four hours before the incident was entered onto the computer database. The hours immediately after incidents of this nature were usually the most crucial; the evidence would be fresh, the trail still hot, and peoples' minds still clear about what they had seen. As hours and then days passed memories of events would change and, though it was not deliberate, it would hamper the investigation. The longer it was left to interview all the protagonists the colder the trail would become.

News of the attempted abduction was passed on to DCI Collins nearly thirty-six hours later. As soon as she read the short version of the report, she knew instinctively that it was her suspect and that this could be a major development in the case.

She immediately called her driver and ordered him to be waiting for her in about twenty minutes outside the divisional headquarters, where she had just finished a meeting with the top brass. There had been two Chief Constables present at the meeting, as well as a Commissioner and a civil servant from the Home Office who was there at the insistence of the Home Secretary himself.

Collins had vigorously defended her record since she had taken charge, and she presented a forceful case. Still the Home Office official had insisted she have an observer, implying that the order had come from the very top. Once her superior officers had heard that, they had quickly cut her legs from under her and agreed to his demands.

Collins was furious, but not surprised. People in the senior positions were nothing more than politicians in uniform, graduates fast-tracked through the system because they were considered good management material. The fact that they had no practical experience of police work, or for that matter any other sort of work, didn't enter the equation. They were part of the system and would follow instruction from their masters as long as it was good for their careers. Now she had a civil servant working on her team, and she didn't want or need that sort of interference. It would badly affect morale knowing they had a spy in the camp. She knew how to handle him though, and placed a call to one of the junior officers on her team. She briefly explained the situation to her colleague, who was only too glad to find enough paperwork to bury the snoop for a month. That would keep him from under Collins's feet while she got on with the real work.

Collins collected her laptop from the incident room and went downstairs to where Paul her driver was waiting in the car for her. The engine was already running and he was eager to have some action. He hated sitting around for hours, but Collins was a good boss and he was very loyal to her, never complaining or whinging about the boredom. Collins appreciated that and made sure she looked after him. She slid in the front seat and, as she fastened up her seatbelt, said:

'Nottingham, Paul, fast as you can.'

She settled into her seat for the drive. It would take about an hour and a half if they were lucky with traffic; she needed to interview 'the one that got away' personally.

She cursed again at the shameful waste of the technology that was available to them; she still had to rely on a couple of village coppers who probably didn't even know how to switch a computer on. Still, the damage was already done now; she let her thoughts wander and soon drifted into a half-sleep, something she had learned to do out of necessity over the years. By the time they reached Nottingham she would be refreshed and ready for what she was sure would be another long day.

Chapter Twenty Five

Amy had left the pub car park and her pursuers behind at high speed as she drove recklessly away from the village. She was filled with outrage, and an intense hatred for the girl who only a few hours before had been the perfect collection piece. How had she allowed herself to be outwitted by that bitch? She shook violently as she drove blindly down the country lanes, unaware of the direction she was taking. She felt her eye and cheek throbbing with pain and screamed in rage at the unfairness of it. Her scream turned to manic laughter as she swerved to avoid colliding with an oncoming tractor in the narrow lanes. She drove on at speed, alternating between outraged screams and manic laughter until gradually her anger began to subside. The pain and rage ebbed away, and in their place grew fear; she heard mother's voice, admonishing her.

'Amy. Amy! Open your eyes and drive straight, you little bitch. Don't you dare harm yourself, Amy; you have work to do. There is no escape for you. I will always find you, wherever you are, and when I do you will go in the cupboard for a month.'

Amy's fear of the cupboard sobered her instantly, and she looked for road signs to guide her back to the hotel. How could she have been so reckless? She had deviated from her usual routine and had very nearly paid the price for her lapse. She had slowed to a reasonable level now and was following the road back to the hotel, thankful that it was night time. The hotel reception was practically deserted as she entered, wearing a pair of dark glasses to conceal her facial injuries. She slipped through the lobby unnoticed, the night porter barely casting a glance in her direction as she ran up the stairway to the safety of her room on the first floor. She didn't want to use the lift in case she met somebody else using it.

She knew that she had to be extremely careful now; that bitch Collins would be down here in no time, poking her nose in everywhere, trying to ruin her chances of finishing the quest. Once she had reached the safety of her room the rage began to return; there on the bed was James. He was the one who had bought her here. He was the one who had put her in jeopardy and nearly ruined everything. When Mother got hold of her, it would be a thrashing and no mistake. Well, soon it would be his turn to answer for his sins, and she would make him pay dearly.

At the noise James awoke and rose from the bed. Rubbing his eyes as he walked towards the en suite bathroom, he never saw the blow coming. Amy's fist crashed into his face, catching him at just the right spot; he fell backwards onto the bed, his mind blank as he lost consciousness.

When James finally came round it was turning light; the warm morning sun was beginning to cast its glow through the large terrace windows. His hand went automatically to his face, feeling the swelling where Amy had landed the blow just below his cheekbone. His head was throbbing, his mind confused. Why had she attacked him like that? His mood had slipped back towards depression, the enjoyment of his long relaxing walk the previous day and his feeling of wellbeing running down the plughole as he looked in the bathroom mirror at his tender face and eye. The bruising was coming to the surface, an ugly, purple and black patch with a small cut across the point of the swelling. He found a flannel and made a cold compress using ice from the fridge; he lay back on the bed, pressing it to his face in order to take the sting away and perhaps reduce the swelling.

He knew he had seen the last of Amy until he got home; she had ruined the break for both of them, leaving him lying unconscious on his own, in a strange room, obviously not caring whether or not he actually woke up. He would settle the hotel bill and return home later in the evening in the hope that Amy would be asleep. He couldn't cope with her moods; not now. His current state of mind did not allow for any unnecessary stress. He had more than enough at the moment with his nightmares, and his work was beginning to suffer. He needed to push Davies as soon as he arrived back to work; he needed Davies to offer him some sort of hope.

Chapter Twenty Six

Davies had been doing a little investigating of his own. He hadn't wanted to go through Collins for fear of compromising James's confidentiality, so he had contacted an old friend, a high ranking police officer who he had helped on occasion with various problems. James had cancelled his appointment so Davies decided to use the time productively. His friend had unrestricted access to the police computer system and was glad to help Davies. He knew that the Doctor was a man to be trusted, and relied upon to be discreet with any information that he may be given.

Nothing unusual had come to light in James's records; he had received a good education at his local grammar school, gaining higher-than-average exam results before going on to graduate in chemistry. His father had died about seven years previously, followed by his mother about a year later. There was nothing to suggest that James was anything but a well-adjusted model citizen; his education and work records were exemplary. He had met Amy a year after his father had died and set up home with her a year after that, at which time his nightmares had started.

Amy was proving rather more difficult. Although she used James's surname, according to the records they had never actually been married. The wedding ceremony had been cancelled at the last minute; the registry office was very meticulous in its record keeping. Davies wondered why they had cancelled the wedding. It wasn't unusual in this day and age to live as common law man and wife, both using the same name; but, because of the circumstances in this case, anything that deviated from the accepted norm would have to be noted.

Amy's records showed that she had been a poor achiever at school, failing to even turn up for her O Level exams. She had been a loner, never mixing with her classmates or getting involved in any sort of activities. Davies could see from the records available that she was a classic case of someone who would invariably end up in trouble. She had drifted from one dead-end job to another, staying only weeks at any one place, until one day she had disappeared, leaving her father frantic and her mother bemoaning the fact that she had never given them anything but trouble.

Amy had been placed on the missing persons' register and after a few months of fruitless appeals had phoned her parents out of the blue. She informed them that she was fine but wouldn't be returning home. She had kept in touch from then on, occasionally speaking to her father by telephone. She moved back home briefly when her father became ill; he had suffered from a degenerative illness for years and finally succumbed to it a few weeks after Amy arrived back home. Her mother was drinking heavily and, not more than a year later, followed Amy's father to an early grave, leaving her alone again. The only record of Amy after that was her proposed wedding to James, which had been cancelled. While there was nothing concrete to point to Amy being disturbed, her records did show that she was not a normal well-adjusted person, and that was enough to rouse Davies's suspicions even more.

Chapter Twenty Seven

Collins and her driver arrived in Nottingham just after lunchtime, and made their way straight to the charity shop. There, two detectives from the local service waited for them to talk through the drama which had unfolded almost forty-eight hours previously. The CCTV system had picked up the suspect when she had entered the shop; Collins hoped that the picture could be enhanced, as it was rather grainy at the moment. Perhaps the computer people could do something with it. Collins spoke to the shop assistant but was satisfied that she had told everything she knew and so she asked the two detectives to lead her to the scene of the incident at the public house in the village.

The village was quiet when they arrived. A typical slice of rural England, she thought, taking in the stone-built houses, with their climbing ivies and colourful flowers. Not the sort of place she would imagine as the scene of a slaughter. They drove past the first two pubs and the hotel, Collins casting an appreciative eye over the traditional architecture. She loved to drive to these villages for lunch when she had the time; it was like a different world to the one she lived in. It brought home to her the squalor of the cities where so many people made their home. This, to her, was the real England; the one that inspired poets, playwrights, and artists to their masterpieces. She wondered how people could accept their lot, living in concrete jungles, riddled as they were with crime and corruption, some of them resembling third-world countries so run-down had they become. Now something twisted had reached out to pollute this place, too, and had very nearly succeeded. She didn't like to think of it.

She was jolted back to reality when the car jumped as it hit a sharp incline in the road. There was a small hump-backed bridge in the centre of the village; they drove over it to reach the pub, which was the last building before the road disappeared round a bend sided with high gorse hedges on top of steep grassy banks.

The pub, when they reached it, was a two-storey black and white coach house. The old stable doors still hung at the far end of the building; the courtyard still retained what looked like the original cobbles. Such a beautiful setting for such an ugly episode thought Collins, as she strode across the car park towards the main entrance, which was covered by climbing roses and bore a weathered sign that proclaimed 'The Traveller's Rest'.

The licensee had kept a room at the back of the pub closed at the request of Collins so that she could conduct her interviews there; she was introduced to him before asking to see the main witness, Michelle. Collins installed herself in the back room, setting up her laptop and ordering coffee while she waited. She read through the information that was available; it wasn't much. Michelle had never been in trouble, had no drink or drugs problems, and had a normal family and friends. Perhaps the killer had come across Michelle accidentally; she wasn't the usual type. Most of the previous victims had had some sort of problems. Maybe she had changed her pattern, got careless; there was a knock at the door and she shouted enter to whoever was there.

A girl walked in; she was about twenty-two, judged Collins, very pretty with curves in all the right places. A stunner, thought Collins. It was only when she looked at the girl's eyes that Collins realised just how stunning she was. They were pale blue, like ice; large and penetrating, they seemed to look right into Collins's mind.

'Hi, I'm Michelle,' said the girl, waking Collins from her trance.

'Hello Michelle, my name is Detective Collins; I would like to speak to you about the incident the other night. I know it must be upsetting for you but we really need to find out everything we can. Every little detail, no matter how small, could be very important to the investigation; this is a very serious incident.'

'I'm fine, detective; it will take more than a weirdo like that to scare me.'

Collins looked at Michelle across the table, wondering how much of that statement was just bravado; not much, she thought. This was a country girl and they tended to be hardy and no-nonsense types. The backbone of England, thought Collins with an inward smile. If they all had this sort of fight then there wouldn't be as many victims.

'Is this anything to do with the girls that have been murdered? I've been reading about it in the papers,' said Michelle, her eyes staring directly into Andrea's.

Collins wasn't often taken by surprise; it was quiet unusual for a victim to be so perceptive and straightforward. She knew it was useless to try and pull the wool over this girl's eyes.

'We have reason to believe that it could be linked to those murders, and that you have had a very lucky escape,' said Collins, waiting for a reaction; she got the one she thought she would.

'It was her who had the lucky escape. If I had got hold of her she wouldn't have gone anywhere,' said Michelle.

Collins had to try hard to stifle a smile. Some people just wouldn't lie down for anybody. They had that indomitable spirit that would carry them through any adversity; here was one such girl, a born fighter and winner.

'You're right; she did have a lucky escape, Michelle. She changed her pattern and very nearly got caught. I'd like you to take me through the whole incident, step by step; just the facts, we can discuss your opinions when we finish.'

Michelle told the story for what must have been the hundredth time. Although she was getting sick of the sound of her own voice she knew how important it was for the police to have every available piece of information, and so was careful to leave nothing out. She knew that Collins was the head detective on the case from reading the newspaper reports, and she was determined to give her all the help she possibly could before another victim was attacked.

Collins questioned her as she recited her story at what she considered relevant points, and soon Michelle had once again finished telling her tale without a single deviation from any of the numerous other statements she had already given.

'When did you first become suspicious Michelle? Was it when you saw her interfere with your drink?' Collins asked.

'No, I thought it strange the way she used my name so easily without prompting,' said Michelle. 'I had only spoken to her briefly; I thought she was too familiar.'

'That instinct probably saved your life,' said Collins.

'I did think I was being paranoid; but it was too much of a coincidence, her turning up here like she did. I don't believe in coincidence,' said Michelle.

'Did you notice anything unusual about her, anything at all; it doesn't matter how small, any detail may help.'

'Not until I thought it over. Her eyes were very fixed when I first met her; staring hard at me, as though she had been surprised at seeing me. She couldn't take her eyes off my face; I just thought that she was attracted to me until after what happened.'

'I suspect she was attracted to you, but not in the way you think. I'm convinced this is the person we've been looking for. She normally picks victims from problem backgrounds or without family and friends, but I think she came across you by accident and couldn't control her urge to have you as her next victim.'

Collins was satisfied that she had gained all she could from this interview; she assured Michelle that a police presence would be around to observe her until the killer had been caught and thanked her for her cooperation. Collins carried out a few more interviews with some of the customers who had been in the pub at the time, including Michelle's friend Moira and the landlord. Accounts varied as they normally do after the passage of time. It was almost amusing, she thought. People always see things different ways; some not wanting to get involved, some wanting to be the hero. The best account undoubtedly came from Michelle herself; she was focused and very clear in both her descriptions and opinions.

Collins finished typing in the details to her laptop and called for her driver; she wanted to be back in Manchester that night because she had a heavy day of meetings the next day. Her first meeting would be with fellow officers to discuss developments, followed by Dr. Davies and Kate Mitchell in that order. They left Nottingham and drove home, Collins continuing her usual habit of catnapping on the long drive. She was fresh and alert by the time Paul woke her as they arrived at her apartment. She would have a couple of hours poring over the files again to see if they looked any different with the latest information entered into them. Before doing that she made a few phone calls, to Task Force HQ and to confirm her appointments for the following day. Finally she settled down to study her files for what seemed like the millionth time.

Chapter Twenty Eight

James had arrived home to find Amy asleep, as he had both expected and hoped. He was at the end of his tether. As if things weren't bad enough, she had to go and make it worse. He looked at his face in the bathroom mirror; there was an ugly red welt high on his cheekbone, surrounded by purple and black bruising. It was still throbbing so he found some ice and lay down on the bed with the ice pack resting over his eye. How would he explain this to Davies, he wondered; he had already asked about Amy. James couldn't understand why, but he would ask Davies at his next consultation. As his breathing became deeper and the pain began to lessen, he drifted off. Amy waited until she was sure he was asleep before she rose from the bed; she went to the wardrobe and dressed before slipping quietly out of the house. She collected her car from the garage and drove slowly out of the end of the road.

Amy crouched, trembling, in the darkness. She could hear mother's voice from the room outside, laughing at her, screaming at her. She had known she would be punished when she had bungled the taking of the latest piece; still, she had hoped it would be a thrashing, and that it wouldn't be the cupboard. This was the place that mother put her when she was really angry with her.

Amy was terrified; there was no light in there, and there wasn't room to stand or move more than a few inches either way. Mother had summoned her to the cellar in that harsh voice, scornful and cruel, and she didn't dare disobey it. When she had arrived she had tried to explain what had happened but mother became angrier as she pleaded not to be locked in the cupboard.

'Get in your cupboard, you worthless little bitch!' Mother screamed at her.

'Please don't, not the cupboard,' Amy had whimpered.

'Get in there now, you ugly little bitch! Nobody wants to see that disgusting face! Get in the cupboard now before you make me sick!' Mother had roared.

Amy, scared witless, had gone to the cupboard in the corner of the cellar and climbed in, closing the door behind her. She sat now, hunched up, her arms wrapped around her legs, hugging herself, trying to draw some comfort from herself. The door wasn't locked but she knew that if she opened it Mother would be there waiting for her, a knotted rope in her hand ready to whip her until she bled. She held the handle on the inside of the door; if it opened even slightly it would be enough to provoke Mother into dragging her from the cupboard by her hair and thrashing her until she passed out.

She could hear the footsteps pacing the floor and Mother's voice, cursing her for her stupidity, screaming profanities at the top of her lungs. All she wanted to do was be a good girl for Mother, but Mother had told her she was rotten to the core and the only thing that would change her was finishing the collection. She had never told Amy when it would be finished, though; or how many pieces she needed to collect or how long it had to go on.

Amy needed to use the toilet but it was unthinkable to ask Mother; the last time she had asked to use the toilet, Mother had let her use it and then forced her head down the pan, nearly drowning her. She had swallowed bleach and her own urine and had been sick for days afterwards. She couldn't control herself any longer and urinated in the cupboard. She hoped Mother wouldn't notice the smell; if she did, it would earn her another beating from her rope.

She was cold and uncomfortable now, and cramp was beginning to creep into her legs. She tried to move but there wasn't enough room. She was feeling pain from being crouched in that position for so long; she had no idea how long it had been, she had lost all sense of time. She could hear her own voice crying like a child, pleading to be let out of this hellhole. Her mouth was dry; she hadn't had a drink in hours. Her head was pounding, she was becoming dehydrated, and she could feel herself drifting into delirium.

Suddenly the door crashed open. Amy was barely conscious; she felt hands grab her hair, tearing it from her head as they dragged her from the cupboard. She didn't dare fight back, even though she knew what was coming; she heard Mother laughing and the swish of the rope as it flailed through the air and landed a stinging blow on her back. The rope rose and fell time and time again, covering Amy's body with red welts which stung mercilessly, and all the while she heard Mother's voice through the haze of pain.

'You will go out and get me my piece tonight, you worthless bitch, or I will whip you for a month, do you understand me?'

Amy could barely speak but she had to make the enormous effort because the beating, she knew, would carry on until she answered.

'Yes, Mother. I understand,' she managed to say, in a hoarse, strained croak. The room was quiet; Amy lay on the floor, unable to move, and lost consciousness at last, releasing her from the torment of the hour-long thrashing.

When she eventually woke, the room was empty. She stirred from her position on the floor, wincing in pain as she slowly dragged herself to her feet and made her way to the trapdoor. She struggled up the steps slowly, her limbs still not recovered from the beating or the long spell of inactivity, and she was just closing the trapdoor when she heard Mother's cackling, manic laugh echoing from the cellar. Her skin crawled; she hoped Mother wouldn't call her back. She hoped she would give her the chance to redeem herself.

Amy made her way to the farmhouse where she ran herself a hot bath; she needed to cleanse herself before she left the farm. She found fruit juice in the fridge and gulped it down greedily, but her mouth was so dry she had difficulty swallowing. It ran down her chin onto her dress, but she was beyond caring now; all she wanted to do was take a long soak in her bath. She went through the motions on autopilot, climbing the stairs and running the water in stiff, jerky movements. She stripped off her soiled clothes and threw them into the washing basket before stepping into the bath and sinking neck deep into the hot, foamy water.

She was asleep in minutes, all pain fading away in the warmth of the water. It was a couple of hours later when she woke; she was shivering, her teeth chattering and her skin wrinkly and cold. She slid into a thick towelling bathrobe and walked downstairs to where the open fire blazed away. She couldn't remember lighting it, but there it was, giving off a comforting, familiar smell of wood smoke and a warm, welcoming glow. She settled down into a comfortable armchair and drifted off into a deep sleep. Her body would recover while she slept. When she woke in the morning she would feel refreshed and ready to resume her quest.

Chapter Twenty Nine

James had dreamed again during the night. He was in total darkness; he couldn't move. It felt like he was in a coffin. There was no air and there was a strong smell of urine. He could hear screaming, a high-pitched wail that seemed to invade every part of his body. Then there was laughter, but not the type of laughter you hear from happy people; this was cruel, manic, tormenting laughter, almost demonic in its tone. It echoed around his head, booming in his ears; and then he could hear voices. He tried straining to hear what they were saying. There was a girl's voice, scared and pleading; it sounded familiar. Over the pleading came the resonant boom of an older voice, a voice of authority; harsh and demanding, unforgiving and spiteful. He had never heard a voice spitting such venom in his life. His head started pounding, his body shaking; cramp was seizing his limbs. He had to get out of here, but he couldn't move.

He felt a door open, and light on his face. His body was dragged with enormous force from his coffin, and he was on the floor. There was a strong smell of damp; the voice was screaming at him. He heard a swish, something sailing through the air, and felt the pain as something struck him across the back. The blows continued, beating every part of his body, and accompanied by that haunting, evil laughter. He could just make out a few words; 'worthless bitch', repeated over and over again. Just when he thought he couldn't take anymore, it stopped just as suddenly as it had started.

He woke up in a cold sweat, his body trembling uncontrollably; he made his way unsteadily to the bathroom, where he stepped into a hot shower. He stayed in the shower until his hands were steady and he felt able to function properly. He dried himself off, dressed, and left the house without breakfast or even coffee. He wanted to get to work and speak to Davies. He felt he was losing his mind completely and he didn't know how much more he could take of this torment.

James was able to see the Doctor within an hour of arriving at work. Davies had left a message at reception for James to make an appointment at the earliest opportunity, and so he found himself on Davies's couch by ten o'clock.

Davies was shocked by James's appearance; he was looking dishevelled and obviously hadn't slept. There were dark rings around his eyes and underneath one eye was a nasty swelling with a small cut across the middle. He had very clearly been in a fight, and by the look of him had come off second best.

'I assume your break didn't go quite as expected then, James,' said Davies, opening the session.

'It was a disaster, Charles. Amy was in a foul mood; she went out for the afternoon and evening on her own and when she arrived back she gave me this. Don't ask me why; she never said a word to me, just attacked me and left me unconscious. When I came round she had left; I don't know how she got home but she left the car. We haven't spoken since. I even left it until late to go home because I knew she would be in bed. I didn't want another confrontation with her when she's in that mood. I don't know where she gets her strength from.'

'Okay James, we will speak about Amy later. First, we will have a session of hypnotherapy, and see if we can get any further with your problem.'

James recounted what he remembered of his dream of the night before, which was not really a great deal. Davies put James in a trance and considered what questions he should ask. From what he had learned about Amy and what James had told him about her behaviour, he was becoming more convinced that she was a very unstable young woman. There was no direct evidence to link her with any of the killings but Davies was fast beginning to think of her as the killer. All of her history and her behaviour pointed in the right direction for the classic case of a serial killer, but he needed something concrete before he could go to Collins with his suspicions. Even then, he would have to be careful how he presented his evidence; nothing collected from his interviews would ever stand up in court. He needed a way to point Collins in the right direction without breaching his confidentiality rules.

During the session James rambled through his usual incoherent memories. It was like building a jigsaw without having all the pieces; Davies had to try and order the events and fill in the gaps. He gently probed James's mind, talking him through the dreams, trying to coax a little more each time, trying to paint a full picture.

James started to become agitated as he mumbled; he was saying something about dark, a box, he was sweating, and Davies could see his hands shaking. He questioned James further. Where was he? What could he see? Was anyone else there?

'Amy,' was the clear reply from James's lips.

Davies was fully alert now. James was becoming more agitated; he started to repeat Amy's name over and over again, and his voice was becoming higher pitched.

'James, where is Amy?' asked Davies.

'In the box, Amy is in the box; please let me out Mother, please don't keep me in here,' James said in a pleading, high-pitched voice.

'Be quiet, you worthless little bitch!' he spat suddenly; his voice had changed to a deeper, harsher tone.

'Why is Mother keeping you in there, Amy?' asked Davies, taking a chance that if he talked to Amy, James might remember more.

'I haven't finished the quest; Mother is angry, she has the

rope, please don't beat me Mother,' pleaded James in that terrified, high-pitched whine.

Davies had heard enough. He had pushed James to the edge; he didn't want to push him over it. He concluded that Amy had been abused badly as a child and that her mother was the abuser. She was on some sort of mission; this all tied in with the classic profile of a sociopath. James was seeing fragments and flashes of Amy's consciousness; he was seeing through her eyes as she carried out her crimes and as she spoke to her abusive mother. It was no wonder he was in such a state, thought Davies; this was enough to push anyone to the limits of their sanity.

Davies woke James from his trance and offered him a cup of tea. He was still shaking and his face was a deathly shade of pale. His lips were vivid red slashes across his face; his eyes were wide and staring, the pupils dilated. Davies gave him a few minutes to calm down before he continued his questioning. James had really let loose this session, and he had given Davies all the cause he needed to confirm his suspicions. Now he had to present it to Collins in a way that wouldn't conflict with the interests of his client. First he needed to ask James a few more questions.

'Have you ever had any psychic experiences, James?' asked Davies.

James looked hard at Davies; this was a doctor, why was he talking like this?

Thinking that he may have misheard Davies, James said:

'Excuse me; I didn't quite catch that, Charles. Could you repeat it please?'

Davies repeated the words he had used slowly and clearly so that James couldn't be mistaken in what he heard.

'I thought that sort of stuff was all nonsense Charles, fortune tellers and all that.'

'Yes, of course. Those sorts of people are just charlatans; they play on peoples' hopes and fears. Nearly all of them are clever fakes but they make a good living out of it.'

'So you're telling me that some of them are genuine?'

'That's exactly what I am telling you, James. It is a widely accepted fact in the scientific community that people can communicate by psychic means; the test results are quite amazing.'

'Well I don't see what this has to do with me; I just want to get rid of these dreams. Why are you telling me about this?'

'Because I think your dreams may not be quite what they seem, James.'

'Don't beat about the bush Doctor, tell me what you mean.'

Davies explained to James about the radio waves in the air all around us and the way the human brain can act as a receiver, just as a television or radio set would, and how if two people tune into the same frequency they will hear or see the same sounds or pictures.

He sat back and watched James closely to see if he understood what he was being told. James was intelligent, but it would still take some time to accept the facts. His face seemed to pale even more; Davies thought he looked like he had been drained of blood, so white had his face become.

'So you're trying to tell me that what I am seeing is actually real?'

'I think it is almost definite that when you sleep, your brain is linked telepathically with someone else's yes,' said Davies.

'But …but that means someone is killing people?'

Realisation was dawning on James. Davies could almost hear his brain whirring away, going back over all his dreams. He watched as James's look of incomprehension turned to one of horror.

'My God, it's that killer I read about in the paper, the Head Hunter! That's what I see in my dreams; heads sat on shelves! I see him killing them, I feel like it's me! My God,' he repeated.

James was losing it; he was starting to babble, the full horror finally registering in his mind. Davies talked to James calmly; he wanted to continue his questioning, but he needed James to be lucid. It was crucial to find out as much as he could before he spoke to Collins.

'When did you first read about the Head Hunter, James?' asked Davies.

'I don't know. A couple of weeks ago, perhaps; I'm not sure, it could have been less, I don't really read the papers much. It was lying on the table; Amy must have been reading it. I noticed it because there was a piece cut out of the paper. Amy doesn't usually take much notice of the news.'

'Do you still have the paper, James?' Davies asked urgently.

'Probably; I put them in a recycling sack. I think they only collect once a month. I saw a Detective Collins was in charge of the investigation. Is that the same Collins who visited you at the lab?'

'Yes. She was here to ask for my assistance with profiling the killer,' said Davies. He leant forward in his chair; it was vital he get hard, physical evidence of what he was now almost certain of.

'Do you think I could have that newspaper from you, James? The one with the piece cut out?'

'If you think it's important, Doctor, then yes, of course you can,' said James.

Davies's mind was racing; if he could obtain that paper he could have a definite link between Amy and the murders. He felt sure that the piece that was missing would be the photo that they had found at the scene of the last murder.

Davies continued his questioning for another half hour; he didn't want to tell James of his suspicions about Amy. He might inadvertently alert her, and that could place James in grave danger. Davies decided that he would call at James's home on his way home this evening to collect the paper and maybe even catch a glimpse of Amy. He was sure it would be safe; she wouldn't do anything to compromise herself if there were two people present. He would make an appointment with Collins for the following morning and present his evidence to her. He dismissed James, giving him a prescription for sleeping tablets; maybe they would help him sleep. He couldn't think how else he was going to help James. As long as the killer was alive, James was likely to have the link with her. He was unsure if his patient would ever be free from the nightmares.

Chapter Thirty

As Davies sat at his desk pondering his dilemma the phone rang, breaking his concentration.

'Hello, Davies,' he said into the hand set.

'Detective Collins is on the phone Doctor, she says it's urgent.'

Collins came on the line; she explained to Davies about the attempted abduction in Nottingham and her concern that the incidents were becoming more frequent. Davies agreed, sharing her concerns, and requested a meeting for the following morning.

He hadn't decided yet how to handle the confidentiality problem but he had decided that tomorrow, he would give Collins the evidence she needed to at least bring Amy in for questioning. He told Collins that he had acquired new material and that he thought it could well give them the name of the killer. He needed to pick up some papers tonight, he had told her, to finish his dossier; he would present his case to her at their meeting in the morning.

Collins was a little more optimistic. She knew that Davies was solid; she had a great deal of respect for him and decided to wait until the morning and trust his judgement to deliver the goods as he had promised.

Collins had been busy speaking to colleagues from all over the country; the cooperation she was getting was far better than it had been in the past. Everybody was making an effort to play the team game; they had all become sick of the criticism and carping that they were receiving from both their superiors and the press. Adversity was clearly pulling them together; people were working on her behalf all across the country, and she felt at last that she was making progress. She was even getting support from some of the press, mainly Kate Mitchell. The others were in full flow, and they were all carrying articles about the 'Head Hunter', wheeling out their so-called experts for their 'professional' opinions, most of which were utter garbage. They were very likely written by bar room lawyers and doctors; sensationalism was the key factor in all of the reports.

Her thoughts were interrupted by the ring of her mobile phone; it was Kate Mitchell. She was extremely excited and Collins could do nothing to calm her down, other than agree that she could come into the incident room in about half an hour with what she said was important information. Mitchell had been a good ally in her hunt for the killer; she had cooperated fully, just as she had promised. She had also put herself at considerable risk by writing such strong articles, in which she had more than once branded the killer a lunatic. She had also used numerous other insults which Davies had suggested; the killer wouldn't see herself as any of those things, Davies had said. It was their best chance to flush her out, making her angry enough to make a major mistake. Collins had placed surveillance on Mitchell's apartment and her office; she didn't want to leave anything to chance. It wasn't beyond the realms of possibility that the killer would try to contact Mitchell directly or even attack her.

Collins gave instructions to the detective who was looking after the Home Office snoop. She was to take him to Nottingham for the day to complete some follow-up interviews; that would keep him out of her hair for a while. She had earlier endured a press conference at which the civil servant had blatantly lied to the press about how long the investigation had been running. He had even suggested that there might not be a link between all of the killings accredited to the 'Head-Hunter'. The Home Office had only recently become aware of the problem, he had said. They didn't interfere with police investigations normally, but in view of the serious nature of this case they were liaising with the task force and offering all assistance to the detectives in charge.

Collins was furious at the way she had been put up as the fall guy already; it had been made clear where any blame, when it was apportioned, would lie, and that would be squarely at her feet. Her snoop from the Home Office left ten minutes before Mitchell walked in the door; it wouldn't be good for Collins if he saw Mitchell in the incident room. She had enough to contend with, without her own side hassling her.

Mitchell breezed into the room like a breath of fresh air. She always had a sense of purpose about her, always seemed to be fully in control and knowing exactly which direction she was going in.

'Good morning, Andrea,' said Mitchell, 'I have something here that might just interest you.'

She was carrying a pile of folders under one arm, her laptop in the other hand.

'Can I use the wall maps, Andrea?' she asked.

'Of course,' said Collins; she was interested now. She could feel the tension emanating from Mitchell. She must think she has something important, thought Collins.

Mitchell fired up her laptop computer and laid the files on a table next to the wall where the large maps of the country were pinned. On each map were a series of coloured pins denoting the place of each murder. The team had searched for hours for some sort of pattern to the killings, but they looked totally random; there was no shape to follow, no straight lines between each murder scene. The locations jumped from one side of the country to another; one killing in Oxford, the next in Chester, the one after in Grimsby. The experts always looked for patterns; quite often the killer would carry out their crimes in certain places that, when linked by drawing lines between them, would show a shape. Maybe a pentangle in cases of black magic or witchcraft rituals; it could be a star sign, a constellation, or a solar system like the earth's, with the killing grounds matching the points of the planets. The moon was a big influence on many of the serial killers who had been studied over the years. All of these things were studied closely to establish a link between the crime scenes, but up to now there was absolutely no pattern they could discern.

Mitchell had found the pattern. She explained briefly to Collins about the search for all the usual patterns, all the star signs and shapes she had studied as had the task force team. After hours of poring over the maps, Mitchell had contacted an old friend and colleague who was a computer expert and asked him to have a look, using his technical know-how. He had run all the usual checks and found nothing, but he prided himself on his ability to solve any problem he was given. He had run hours of tests to try and establish some sort of pattern, and had finally found it. His second-to-last test had involved numbers, and his last test was with letters; that was where he had struck gold.

Mitchell took a black marker pen in her hand and turned to the largest map on the wall. The lines between the crime scenes had been marked from place to place in order of dates. As each killing had been discovered, the line had extended to the new scene. It resembled a spider's web, nothing more than a mishmash of inter-crossing lines.

'Where we have been going wrong is in looking for a single shape or item,' Mitchell said, half-turning to face Collins.

'What we have found are three separate shapes; three letters, to be precise. We used the computer to superimpose letters on the map, starting with A of course. All we had to do was alter the size of the letter and move it around until it matched with any of the crime scenes.'

Collins was growing both impatient and excited at Mitchell's presentation. 'Right, well let's see what you came up with then, Kate,' said Collins.

Mitchell drew as she spoke; starting at Newcastle in the north, she drew a straight line to Liverpool. She then drew a line from Newcastle to Louth, just south of Grimsby. Next, she drew another line from Preston to Kingston-upon-Hull.

Collins was staring at a large letter A on the map; along the lines of the thick black marks of the pen were coloured pins, each one marking a murder scene. Bradford and Leeds stood on the cross bar of the A from Preston to Kingston. Each one of those towns or cities had suffered a killing. On the left side of the A, in between Newcastle and Liverpool, were Ripon and Preston, all murder scenes. On the right side of the A were Newcastle, Durham, Middlesbrough, Beverly, Kingston, Grimsby, and Louth. There were more killings on that side but there were also more towns; the left side of the A missed out a lot of the cities and towns because it was running through the countryside.

'We wouldn't have seen it because we were following the murders by date, so there was no apparent pattern; but the killer knew the end result. She must have done it like that to throw us off the trail' said Mitchell.

She started drawing another line from Wrexham to Lancaster, then on to Sheffield, and then on to Bridlington in the north. From there she continued, drawing the line southwards again, through Grimsby down as far as Boston in Lincolnshire. This time the lines formed an M. The third set of lines formed a Y, running from Southampton to Oxford and then up to Oswestry on the left branch of the Y and King's Lynn in Norfolk at the top of the right branch. Mitchell wrote on the white board next to the maps the letters AMY.

'That's her name,' she said to Collins, 'she's trying to tell us her name just like Doctor Davies said she might. She wants us to catch her.'

Collins stood speechless for a moment, taking it all in.

'That's damn good work, Kate; and I agree with you that she probably wants us to catch her. But remember; she has more than one personality, and the other one will be doing everything in her power to throw us off the track. She's also trying to confuse us. She's toying with us.'

'I realise that, but surely this can be used in some way?'

'Of course, it's a breakthrough; we spent months studying that data and never came near to finding that pattern.'

'How can you use it then, Andrea? How are you going to hunt her down with just a Christian name?'

'First, we contact the registrars of births and deaths in all the counties. Their records are all kept on disc now. We can give an approximate age range and ask them to search their records; I don't think Amy is a really common name so we could be in luck.'

'I don't think I have ever known anyone called Amy,' said Mitchell; 'you might have a point there.'

'I hope so, Kate; I'm getting extreme pressure from above about this case. This could be the break we need.'

Collins picked up the phone and spoke to Administration, giving them the details of what she required and placing an urgent tag on her request. She wanted the results on her desk by late afternoon she told them, before hanging up to resume her discussion with Mitchell.

'I have a meeting with Davies in the morning; maybe you would like to be here and explain what you found to him.'

'Thanks, Andrea. I will be here for nine, or is that too early?'

'No, we can go over things before Davies gets here; he's due in at ten.'

Mitchell left the office; she had work to do at her own. They had agreed that the suspect would be named as Amy in the morning edition of her publication. Mitchell had agreed to write another article about the killer and to attack her ruthlessly; she had no qualms now about angering Amy. She could see that it was necessary to draw her into the open, regardless of the risks involved to any other potential victims. The killings could go on for years if they didn't stop her. They had to play the game and take chances with people's lives. One more life lost could save many more from being lost, if they could anger Amy enough to make a major mistake as she had done in Nottingham.

She arrived at her office and put the editor on alert for her latest story; it would be front page and it would be scathing in its criticism of Amy. The office was buzzing already as news of her story was circulated amongst her colleagues. She sat at her desk and started to compose the article; it would take her a few hours to get it right. She wanted it to be perfect and that took time, so she settled down in her swivel chair with a pot of coffee at hand and penned what she hoped would be the lure to draw the killer into the arms of the police.

Chapter Thirty One

Amy arrived in Huddersfield late in the evening; she had planned to come here earlier to look around for another piece for her collection. She must have it tonight; she couldn't endure another beating from Mother like the one she had suffered in the early hours of the morning.

She had been delayed by an unexpected visitor at her home; she hadn't expected to see Davies at her door and was thrown off balance. She knew who he was, and that as well as working with James he was helping the police with their search for her. His name had appeared in Mitchell's rag along with Collins, the DCI in charge of the case.

She knew as soon as he looked at her that he suspected her; he wasn't a professional police officer, and his face told the story. She had handled him quite well, she thought as she parked her car in a passageway behind a nightclub. She was taking a chance tonight; she didn't have time to search for too long for the best piece.

Mother wanted it tonight, so she would have to take the best she could find at such short notice. She tried a couple of pubs and didn't see anything worthy of her collection but struck lucky in the club she entered as the last resort; she was running late and was feeling the pressure. There at the bar as she walked in was a girl on her own. She had been crying; her eye make-up was smudged where she had rubbed her eyes. Amy sat next to the girl at the bar.

'Are you okay?' she asked.

The girl sniffed and looked at Amy.

'I'm fine, thanks. My boyfriend stood me up, but it's his loss; stuff him.'

'Good for you,' said Amy, 'there's plenty more out there. Don't let a man ruin your life for you.'

'Don't worry, I won't,' said the girl.

Amy was studying the piece carefully. Yes, she would do, she thought; not the prettiest but still very attractive. She would sit well next to the redhead, a nice contrast in hair colour with her nearly black, thick, wavy hair.

Amy paid for drinks for both of them and her piece was soon relaxed in her company; they had a few more drinks before Amy suggested that she gave her a lift home. The piece readily agreed and left the club with Amy not long after. Amy drove towards the moors; her piece lived on a small farm a few miles from the town centre. Amy pulled over at a lay-by and got out of the car.

'Come on, lets sit in the moonlight,' she said to the piece. 'Have a drink of this.'

The girl took the bottle from Amy and swigged a large mouthful of the drink. Amy let the piece chatter on to her as they sat on a wooden bench overlooking the valley spread before them, an eerie silver glow bathing the landscape. Not long now, thought Amy as she waited for the drugs to take effect.

The piece slid down from the bench within minutes of taking the drug; Amy didn't have time tonight to choose her place for the ritual. There was a sign post set back from the road, with name plates sticking out in opposite directions; it would have to do, she thought. She would leave the waste in full public view; if those people wanted to interfere in her business she would interfere in theirs. If a member of the public found the off-cuts of her piece here, there would be outrage in the media. They thought they were smart but they weren't as smart as her. She chuckled to herself as she dragged the girl to the post and tied her hands with the blue nylon rope from her holdall. She threw the rope over the arms of the sign post and hoisted her up until she was in the crucifixion pose.

Amy took her knife from the holdall and cut away the upper clothing from the piece; she didn't have time to waste tonight. She plunged the knife into the girl's ribcage, with the blade vertical so that it broke the ribs either side of the blade; she sawed up and down, then across. She soon had a hole cut large enough to reach into and take the heart. She hacked at the arteries hurriedly until the heart, still spurting blood in large quantities, fell away into her hand. She tossed it into the plastic bag in the holdall and picked up her meat cleaver. As she straightened up to take hold of the piece's hair, she was surprised to see its eyes open wide as though in surprise. They stayed open for a few seconds, staring unseeing at a point beyond Amy's shoulder before closing for the last time.

It had taken less than two minutes. Amy was intrigued by the way the eyes had opened after she had cut out the piece's heart; she stared at the now closed eyes. Her mind was wandering again; she had to hurry, it was getting late. She grabbed a handful of hair and yanked the head back.

Her cleaver hacked at the neck with a sweet chopping sound; blood spurted from the arteries it had severed. Amy felt the warmth of the fresh blood running down her face; it ran down to her chin and dripped onto her dress. Her hands were also soaked in blood, warm and sticky; she tasted the sweet saltiness as it ran over her lips.

She could feel the excitement growing through her body; she licked her lips, savouring the sweet taste. She could almost smell it, she thought. She was very tempted to take the heart from the holdall and eat it now. She could barely contain herself; her body was trembling, and she felt ecstatic as she licked the blood from her hands. She was losing control; she reached down to the holdall for the heart, her eyes wild and glazed, and her hair blowing in the cool night breeze. Her face was covered in blood; she was higher than she had ever been. As she grabbed the heart she froze.

'PUT THAT BACK YOU WORTHLESS LITTLE BITCH!' she heard Mother scream at her.

'If you do that you go in the cupboard for a month!'

Amy dropped the heart; her excitement was replaced with cold fear, and she backed away, looking for Mother. She looked slowly around her, waiting for a blow to land from somewhere, and she cringed as the voice boomed again.

'Get the piece and bring it to me! Now, now, NOW!'

Amy covered her ears, but it was no use; the voice would penetrate the thickest walls, she knew. There was no escape. She picked the cleaver up from where it had fallen on the grass and started hacking frenziedly at the torso of the dead piece; the head was severed after a few blows, and rolled from the neck to fall at Amy's feet, with a dull thud as it landed on the hard ground.

Amy grabbed the head and threw it into the holdall; she put the holdall in the car boot and stumbled around to the car door. She fumbled with the keys as she tried to start the engine; she was shaking badly. She managed to calm herself enough to start up the engine and, without even looking for any oncoming traffic, she hurled the car onto the road. The gravel from the lay-by kicked up behind her wheels with a tearing sound as she raced away at speed towards the M62 and the safety of her gallery.

The first vehicle to pass the lay by in daylight was a milk delivery van; the driver pulled in and left his cab to see what was tied to the signpost. As he neared the body his heart started pounding as he realised what he was seeing; he reached for his mobile phone as he stared transfixed at the horribly mutilated, headless corpse. Before he could dial 999 he was on his knees, vomiting; it was a few minutes before he could compose himself enough to make the call to the police. Even then his account of what he had stumbled across was rambling and barely coherent; he was clearly in shock.

The operator had heard it many times before. She talked to him calmly and professionally as she typed in a flash message for police headquarters. She knew straight away that it was the Head Hunter and she knew where to send the message for the quickest response. She talked to the van driver until she heard the wail of the siren down the line and then ended the call. She took the tape from the recorder; she knew that someone would be here to collect that one very quickly. How long would it take before they caught this lunatic she thought as she sealed the tape in an envelope and marked it for attention of DCI Collins.

Chapter Thirty Two

Collins had been woken early from a disturbed sleep; the stress was getting to her. She knew she wasn't sleeping well; her eyes were dark underneath, and she felt drained of energy. Her pager went off with what seemed liked a deafening screech in the quiet of her bedroom. She knew it would be another killing; nobody would call her at this time of morning unless it was absolutely essential. She called the Task Force HQ where her junior officers were already working, collating the details from the latest incident. She was given a rundown of the information available and headed for the shower, switching the kettle on as she passed through the kitchen.

She showered and dressed before going back to the kitchen. As she made coffee she made a call to Mitchell. Their appointment with Davies would have to wait, but she might as well have Kate along; they could discuss things on the way to the crime scene. Kate was proving to be very useful to the investigation. She remembered to call Davies's office; she would be delayed, but would speak to him as soon as possible she said into the answering machine. Her phone rang twice before cutting off; that would be Paul. He always seemed to know when he was needed, no matter the time of day or night; he was always there. Collins appreciated his dedication; she would have to make sure he had time off when this investigation was finished. She knew only too well how work could overtake your life so completely.

They picked Mitchell up and headed along the M62 towards Huddersfield, talking as they travelled. Mitchell had picked up a copy of the morning paper and she showed Collins the front page story. Even Collins was surprised by the strength of the article. She wondered if Davies would think it was a bit over the top, a little too provocative; but as the latest events had shown, the killer didn't need much provocation to strike again.

They arrived at the crime scene to find the local police struggling to control the gathering posse of news people and onlookers. Collins ordered the road be closed immediately and that all persons not connected to the investigation should be removed from the scene. There were the usual grumbles from the media about censorship and public interest, but Collins didn't give a damn about their whining; she had important work to do.

The birds had been at work on the body; she could see some large black crows a few yards away, picking at chunks of torn flesh they had ripped from the wounds to the dead girl. Collins and Mitchell taped the area off, something that should have been done as soon as the first officers arrived; with so many people turning up it had been difficult for them to establish a proper crime scene exclusion zone.

The forensic team had just arrived and, after setting up a screen to mask the body from prying eyes, began the work of scouring the area for any clues or small piece of evidence. Part of the team worked on the body, checking under finger nails to see if there was any flesh from the killer. It was always a possibility that the victim had fought back; the last intended victim had, and it was only a matter of time before one of them fought hard enough to injure the killer. Of course, that depended on whether she had administered the drugs to them. Once they were drugged the chances of survival were nil. The killer had shown no mercy to any of her victims.

The head of the forensic team beckoned her over.

'Slightly different this time, Andrea,' he said to Collins.

Collins stood only a couple of feet from the body; there was already a putrid smell to it. The warm weather would soon rot the flesh if it was left too long in the open. This killing looked even more savage than the others; the wounds around the torso seemed to be larger and more numerous than those to the other victims. Where the head had been removed there were many more gashes than in previous cases. Was the killer becoming agitated? That was a strange thing to think; most people would consider the killer a very agitated person already. It was really quite surreal, trying to follow the thinking of a psychopathic serial killer, being expected to know what they would do or think next. How could anyone get into the head of someone like this?

She remembered Davies telling her that they would never really understand why the killers behaved in the way they did. All they could do was theorise, based on evidence they collected and the limited interviews they managed to secure with killers. Once they were caught they usually clammed up; it had been proven in most cases that they just refused to acknowledge any wrong doing.

She interrupted her thoughts to speak to Anderson, the head forensic scientist.

'Why is it different, Steven? Do you mean she's becoming more frenzied?'

'Well, yes; you can obviously see for yourself that the wounds are more random and probably inflicted more hurriedly than previously. The main difference here though is that this girl was almost certainly still unconscious from the effect of the drugs when she was killed. All the others were killed after they had regained consciousness.'

'How can you tell that?' asked Collins.

'We tested for drugs first; the same substance has been used again, but the blood flow this time is different. When the victim is conscious the heart is racing and pumping blood around the body very fast. The body also produces adrenalin when a person is agitated or in a state of fear. The adrenalin traces are low in this case which suggests that the victim didn't know what was happening to her. The blood in an agitated, conscious person would drain much quicker and spurt further than we can see here, due to the increase of pressure caused by the increased heart rate.'

'So what does that tell us?'

'Probably that she was rushing for some reason; she may have been worried about being disturbed or she might just be losing it altogether. It was a particularly frenzied attack, much more so than in any of the other killings.'

'If she was concerned about being disturbed she could have chosen a better place to carry out the attack,' said Collins.

'I'd agree with that; could she be working to a timetable? Maybe she is running out of time for some reason. It's hard to even guess how she thinks.'

'If only we knew,' said Andrea. 'At least she wouldn't have suffered as much as the others, if that's any consolation.'

'Try telling that to the family,' said Anderson with a pained expression on his face, as he went back to work on the remains of the latest victim.

Mitchell had been listening to the conversation while she studied the body in detached fascination; she was learning quickly to cope with the horror of murder and found herself able to think clearly. She too was trying to imagine the thoughts that must go through the killer's mind as she committed her heinous crimes; but, like Collins, she couldn't even begin to comprehend the reasons behind those twisted thoughts.

'Can we do any more here Andrea, or shall we find somewhere to get some coffee?' she asked.

'No, we can't do anything here; let's go into town and get some breakfast. It's going to be a long day; we can come back when the incident room is set up and the rest of the team members arrive,' said Collins.

The two women turned away from the corpse and walked in silence to their waiting vehicle, each lost in their own thoughts.

Chapter Thirty Three

James Elliot was dreaming again. He was in the cellar where the heads were kept; the air was damp-smelling and warm. He was standing in front of the vase, the eyes staring at him, piercing and evil, almost hypnotic. He held the head up in front of him. It was a young girl; her eyes were shut, unlike the others that adorned the shelves around the room.

His head was light, a dizzy feeling creeping over him; images were flashing before his eyes. He saw the cleaver rise and fall with sickening sounds as it cut into flesh. He saw the gaping hole in the girl's body, and the heart held in his hand, blood dripping through his fingers. He was terrified; his stomach knotted, his throat dry. An image of Davies flashed through his mind. He was talking to him, pleading with him, but there was no sound; just the silent mouthing as if Davies was trying to tell him something. He listened hard, but still he couldn't hear what Davies was trying to say.

His legs were rooted to the spot; he couldn't turn and run even if he wanted to.

He smelt burning rubber, heard the screech of car wheels on gravel as he drove away at high speed. There was stickiness on his face, he touched it and saw blood on his fingertips. He was lifting the trapdoor in the floor of the barn and then he was in the cellar; he felt the nausea rise as he saw his slender feminine hand lifting the heart from the holdall, and bringing it towards his mouth. He could feel his teeth chewing through the raw heart, blood trickling down his chin.

He was back at the lay-by and he heard the thud of the head as it spilled from the girl's shoulders onto the hard baked earth. His mind was racing through images, jumping from one dream to another; he could hear the voices again, and he felt his own mouth moving, and a pleading, high-pitched voice, begging not to be punished. Then came the harsh, cruel voice, ridiculing Amy again, telling her she was useless, worthless. Why was the voice talking to Amy, he thought; where was Amy?

His mind was confused, his senses screaming for release; he looked round the room, trying to see where Amy was. All he could see were the heads, the eyes still wide and staring, looking at him accusingly. He could smell a familiar scent but wasn't quite sure what it was; it reminded him of the lab at work. It came to him as he saw an image of a bottled specimen standing on a shelf at the lab; it was formaldehyde. The heads must be soaked in it to preserve them he thought as he watched the involuntary movements of his hands. Soaked in blood, they were still holding what was left of the heart in them while he chewed on the piece in his mouth. But they weren't his hands, he knew; they were women's hands, slender and strong, he could feel the strength in them as they gripped the heart. It wasn't his mouth; he was seeing and feeling all of these things through somebody else's senses and eyes. He heard the voice calling Amy again; it was mocking her.

'How could you be so stupid, you little bitch? You know they have to look at me! Find me another one or you'll be in the cupboard!'

He could feel the fear like it was his own; he could feel the sweat running down his back, his heart pounding in his chest. His breathing was laboured, and he could feel the panic rising up through his stomach to his chest. He felt like a big weight was crushing him; he was struggling to breathe now and his head was becoming light. He knew he was going to pass out if the pressure increased any more.

Suddenly he was awake, sitting up rigidly in his bed, his eyes bulging from their sockets with fear. His hands were shaking badly, his chest heaving as he gasped for breath; he rose on unsteady feet and staggered to the bathroom. He supported his weight by leaning on first the bed rails, and then the dressing table as he made his way erratically to the shower. He turned on the shower and stood under the cool streams of water; he had to lean on the cubicle door to steady himself. He felt so weak he could barely stand without support.

It took another ten minutes before he felt steady enough on his feet to leave the shower and dry himself. He found some casual clothes and dressed, pulling his tee shirt over his head as he made his way downstairs to the phone. He called work and asked for Dr. Davies's secretary; he had to have an appointment that day. She informed him that the doctor hadn't arrived at work that morning, but if he arrived or called she would get the doctor to call him immediately.

James wasn't happy that he couldn't see Davies; he needed to talk to him urgently. He hoped that Davies would call him back. James went to the drinks cabinet and took out a bottle of malt whiskey. He poured a large shot into a small glass, threw it back quickly, and poured another large measure. Hopefully the whiskey would give him some relief, he thought; he gulped at the drink as if it was water. He had soon consumed three quarters of the bottle and was very drunk. He was slouching in his armchair, feeling a warm glow as the whiskey took effect. He felt his eyes closing, and quickly slipped into an alcohol induced sleep. At least he would be free from his nightmares while he was in his drunken stupor.

Chapter Thirty Four

Collins and Mitchell had been busy all day. Collins had conducted interviews with family and friends of the dead girl while Mitchell sifted through the statements as they came into the incident room one at a time. It was fairly tedious work, but she had two team members typing and filing the reports before she read them. They were good company, she had found; she tried not to intrude into their space too much, and they seemed to respect her. They knew she was putting the investigation before her personal ambitions and that went down well with people who usually found journalists to be self-centred, self-righteous gold diggers.

There was no forensic evidence worthy of note at the murder scene. They had the casts of the tyres from the vehicle, and a few shoe prints, but without some blood or DNA samples they would struggle to make any sort of identification of the killer. The only sample they had collected was from a previous murder, a single hair that had come from a wig; it didn't help much in their search.

Collins had asked Mitchell to contact Davies to arrange a meeting for the following afternoon; all the evidence would be collated by then, ready to present to the Doctor for his assessment. She was eager to learn what Davies had discovered, but suspected that he might have found the same pattern as Mitchell had found. The name on its own didn't mean much, but already they had a list of girls named Amy and were interviewing them all. Unfortunately, they didn't have as much manpower as she would like. Although there were only a few hundred girls named Amy in the target area where the highest concentration of murders had occurred, it would still take them days and even weeks to eliminate them all from the inquiry.

Mitchell was unable to contact Davies; she had the same response as James had received. The doctor hadn't turned in for work and had not been in contact but as soon as he made contact his secretary would ask him to call Collins to confirm a meeting for the following afternoon. His diary was fully booked, but she was sure he would be able to shuffle it for Collins.

Mitchell passed the message on to Collins; she would have preferred to see him today, but it would just have to wait, she thought. Mitchell's mobile phone rang; it was the office.

'Hello, Mitchell here,' she said into the mouthpiece.

'Hi Kate, it's your favourite editor,' came the reply from the familiar voice.

'Hi boss, what can I do for you?' Kate asked. She wasn't in the mood for banter; her head was aching from the tension of work, and she was feeling very irritable.

'Your article seems to have drawn a response from our friend; she's sent you a message,' said Mitchell's editor. 'Have you got a fax there?'

'Yes, please send it over; and put the original in a plastic bag, forensics will want to run tests on it.'

Mitchell gave him the number and assured him that she was fine.

'Just a little tired,' she told him before she ended the call and walked to the fax machine in the corner of the room. She poured a glass of chilled water from the dispenser next to the fax while she waited for the message to come through. She wondered what it would say and why the killer was using her as a messenger. The fax rang and she heard the electronic handshake as it connected to the office line. It was a single page and had a hand-drawn picture on it. It was of a chicken. It was obviously meant to be running; although the art work wasn't good, it still managed to capture the movement. The chicken had no head, and underneath the crude sketch were the words 'From Amy Jayne.'

Mitchell stared at it; what did it mean? Amy was taunting her; that much was obvious. She was gloating because she knew that they were no closer to catching her than they had been six months ago. Mitchell was angry; she showed the message to the two detectives in the mobile incident room, and she could see that they were angry as well. Collins arrived from her interviews and cursed when she saw the single sheet with the headless chicken on it. She was feeling the stress as well.

'She's going to get careless,' she told Mitchell and her team members. 'She's getting far too cocky; she's already made a major blunder at Nottingham, and we know she was rushing at Huddersfield. Her ego is getting the better of her; she thinks she's too clever for us all, and that will be her downfall,' concluded Collins.

Mitchell wondered how she could stay so positive; this police work really was hard, and it was like going round in circles. She had only been involved for a few weeks and it felt like a lifetime already. She wondered whether she should admire these people or pity them for their dull, tedious existence.

'Right,' said Collins to her team, 'it's been a long one, let's call it a day. Who fancies a drink over the road before they head home?'

'Sounds good to me, boss,' her detectives said in unison.

'Me too,' said Mitchell.

The four of them, along with Collins's driver Paul, walked across the road to the small public house situated on the junction of a crossroads. They found a table in a quiet corner while Collins went to the bar to order drinks. She knew what each of them would have; this had become quite a ritual for them since they had been working together on this case. They could relax a little, share a few jokes and forget all about work for a brief spell; tomorrow would come soon enough. Collins and

Mitchell were both wondering what new horrors the new day would bring as the team members relaxed and laughed at a crude joke. They deserve it, thought Collins; she knew that their marriages suffered in this line of work, and any little relief they could get was a bonus for them. They stayed for a couple of hours. All of them except Paul were quite merry by the time they left the pub, and they all slept as Paul drove them over the moors onto the M62 towards Manchester and their waiting beds.

Chapter Thirty Five

Collins arrived in the office late; she had struggled to get out of bed this morning. She had a hangover and was drinking pints of water to stem the dehydration as best she could. She had just got rid of the Home Office snoop; she had sent him to do some checks at the registry office in central Manchester. He had no idea that all of that information had been forwarded already, it would keep him busy for the next two or three days, and he would be able to report back to his masters that he was doing a good job. How the hell did the country function, she asked herself, with bumbling idiots like him involved in running it?

Collins placed a call to the research centre; she still hadn't heard from Davies, and she needed him in this afternoon to give a briefing to some of her senior officers. He hadn't turned in for work again, his secretary told Collins.

'It isn't like him at all; I'm really quite worried about him.'

Collins told the woman that she had Davies's home number and would try him there.

'But I've already tried,' she said, with a worried note to her voice.

'Well I'm sure he's alright; he probably has flu, there's a lot of it going around at the moment,' said Collins, trying to reassure the woman. She knew how some of these secretaries could be overprotective of their bosses, especially if they were middle-aged single men; they liked to mother them.

She returned to her paperwork. If Davies couldn't make it she would have to do the briefing herself. She hated briefing the top brass. They seemed to have nothing better to do than ask inane questions that even a child wouldn't ask for fear of sounding stupid. Still, she couldn't get out of it, so she buried her head in her files and started to write up a profile and progress report that would pass the test. She had a few calls during the morning but managed to complete her presentation with plenty of time to spare; she left it on her desk, and called to her junior watch officer that she was going out for lunch. She needed to breathe some fresh air; after her late night and then being stuck in the office all morning, she was feeling decidedly ill. A good brisk walk by the side of the canal would clear her head.

Kate Mitchell was feeling just about the same way as Collins was feeling; none of them were used to large amounts of alcohol, and after a couple of stiff drinks they should really have stopped. It must be the stress, thought Mitchell; it makes you want to lose your sense of reality, even if only for a while. It was an escape from the pressure of working on a case like this one. The mail boy called her name across the office.

'Delivery for you, Kate; do you want it at your desk?'

'Yes please, Tony,' replied Mitchell. She watched as the office junior made his way through the aisles between the desks, carrying a fairly large parcel. She was expecting a delivery; she had ordered a new mini CD system online and given the office as the delivery address. They would never catch her if they tried to deliver at home. The boy placed it on her desk with a smile and left her to open it.

The package had been delivered by a national carrier, she saw; she slit the tape which held the box closed using her penknife. She couldn't wait until she got home; she didn't buy many luxuries, but when she did get something new she got as excited as a child at Christmas. She took her time opening the box, just as she always had done as a child; it seemed to her that the longer you took in opening the box, the more pleasurable it felt. She laughed at herself as she lifted the lid from the box; she lifted the flat piece of polystyrene that was underneath the lid, and stared down at the contents of the box.

The first thing to hit her was the smell; a rancid, rotten meat kind of smell. She felt the nausea rising; her eyes were seeing but her brain wasn't registering what she saw. For a few microseconds her world stood still, her smile frozen on her face; she heard someone screaming, a terrified sounding scream, very near. She realised that her mouth was open and the sound was emanating from her own lips. Her brain finally caught up with her sound and vision, and her awareness kicked in; she was looking down into the box, and in the box was the head of her colleague, Doctor Charles Davies, deceased.

She reeled back from her desk, falling backwards as she caught her legs on the chair; she landed on her side in a heap. She clawed her way onto her hands and knees but was too weak to rise; she felt her stomach heave and she emptied the contents all over the carpet. As her colleagues rushed to her aid she was still screaming and heaving alternately, the horror was too much, she felt the blackness wash over her as she lost consciousness.

Collins arrived at the newspapers offices within twenty minutes of Mitchell opening the box; she had received an urgent message on her pager, and after making a call on her mobile phone had been in a car and on her way within two minutes. Uniformed officers had sealed the area and were preventing anyone from entering the whole floor which the news offices were situated on. That couldn't happen; she ordered that just the area round Mitchell's desk was to be cordoned off. The evidence, if there was any, would be in or on the box. She couldn't close down a newspaper production line for anything. That really would be the end of her career.

She could smell it before she reached the desk; the stink of fresh vomit pervaded the air, but the overpowering odour was the stench of rotting flesh. She had smelt it before and knew that there was no mistaking that sickly, sweet smell. She walked the last few feet to the desk slowly; she didn't want to look into that box. She knew what was inside it, and she was filled with horror that Davies had become a victim of Amy. He was such a kind, thoughtful man; he didn't deserve this. This was personal; he was dead because he had helped Collins with the investigation.

Was the information he had told her about conclusive, then? Maybe he had discovered the identity of Amy; but he didn't seem like someone who would grandstand. If he was getting close to Amy and had then been murdered, did that mean that Amy knew he was close? And if she did, then how did she know? The next logical thought was that Davies actually knew her, and she had some insight into the investigation; or maybe she knew someone who was close to the investigation.

The thoughts were racing around Collins's mind as she reached the box, still sat on top of Kate Mitchell's desk. She braced herself and looked down at Davies's face. His sightless eyes looked up at her; the expression was one of surprise. That was odd; why was he surprised? If he knew the killer surely he wouldn't have such a look on his face. Collins' thoughts were racing; she set them aside as the forensic team arrived and began taking photos. When they had finished they sealed the box and carried it from the building, to carry out the tests at the pathology lab. Collins had asked them to establish whether it was the same weapon which had been used in other killings. She wouldn't be disappointed; she would discover within the hour that it was the same cleaver that had decapitated the last four victims.

Collins left with the forensic team; she had been summoned to Headquarters by her Chief Constable. There would be big repercussions now, because Davies was such a well known figure in the academic world. Her bosses would think he was more important than the other victims, because he was part of the establishment. She didn't have time to talk to Mitchell; her friend had been sedated by a doctor who had been called to the office. She wouldn't be fit to interview until the morning; the rest would do her good thought Collins as she left the building with her team. Mitchell would be safe; Collins had stepped up surveillance on her apartment and was satisfied that no one would get within a hundred yards of the building without being spotted and questioned by one of her officers. She jumped in the back seat of her waiting car, playing the recent events over in her mind as they sped towards Headquarters just a few miles across town.

Chapter Thirty Six

Amy had been busy all day. First she had driven into central Manchester, and posted another picture to Collins; she would receive it first thing in the morning. She had gone to the trouble of putting a first class stamp on the envelope; she wanted it delivered quickly. She wished she could have seen Collins's face when she looked in the box; what a picture that would have made. She was busy now, disposing of Davies's body; his head had been of no use to her, other than to taunt Mitchell and Collins with. Still, it had worked out even better than she thought it would; his useless head had, after all, served a purpose.

She had her plastic apron on and her latex surgical gloves, and was chuckling to herself; even James had his uses, she thought. He had a constant supply of gloves from the lab, and access to the drugs she needed for her quest. She had just finished dismembering Davies's body with the small electric chainsaw that James had purchased last year. She had cut the body into the smallest pieces that she could manage; it had taken her longer than expected because he was quite a large man. She had dumped his body in the bath after decapitating him while he lay on the kitchen floor. She was glad she had taken his head off first; he had been so heavy, and she might not have managed to lift him with the added weight of his head.

Her other problem had been the bath. She realised that the chainsaw would damage the bath if she cut straight through the remains, and the last thing she wanted was to have to buy a new bath; she had seen them advertised in a magazine and they were very expensive. She wasn't hard up but she didn't like spending money if she could avoid it; so she found two old planks of wood in the garage and laid them on top of the bath, with the body lying on top of the planks. It worked perfectly; the bath had suffered no damage and the body was now cut into small pieces. The only problem she had encountered was the blade of the saw sticking in the timber now and again. She washed the chain in the sink and studied it; there didn't seem to be any damage, and if there was she could have it sharpened at the lawnmower shop in town for a few pounds.

She was quite pleased with her day's work; she dragged the refuse bin with the meat in it through to the kitchen, where she had set up her mincing machine. It was on the side of the sink so that the outlet was protruding over the bowl. She switched on the machine and started feeding pieces into the top; the motor whirred louder as the first pieces of bone, flesh and sinew were dragged down into the blades to be crushed and minced.

It was a long, tedious job; she had to feed the machine piece by piece until it was gone. It was a pity she hadn't had time to just dump the body. It would have saved her a lot of work; her arms were beginning to tire. Damn men, she thought; they were never anything but trouble. She pushed the minced meat into the waste disposal unit of the sink; it would all be washed away down the drains, and the rats would have a feast tonight.

She watched as the machine churned out the mince; it looked just like the stuff you could buy at the butchers. What a pity she didn't have a market stall or shop, she mused; she could have sold the mince and made enough to keep her car topped up with petrol for a week or two. Well, she couldn't think of everything; but she would bear that in mind if she ever had to mince someone else.

She finally finished the mincing after what seemed like hours; now she had to clean up. She was covered in blood; her face was streaked with a mixture of blood and sweat, her arms red all the way up to her elbows. She spent an hour cleaning the kitchen, and then the bathroom, until everything was sparkling and fresh. She put Davies's clothes in a black refuse sack. She would take them to the farm and burn them in the wood-burning stove in the kitchen. At last she could shower; she stood under the piping-hot spray from the shower head and scrubbed herself from head to toe. She was smiling as she washed herself, and humming her favourite song. She was happy; her quest would soon be over. Mother was going to be delighted when she saw the latest piece she had collected, and she would be proud of Amy's initiative in dealing with Davies.

He could have been trouble; Amy knew as soon as she opened the door to him that he suspected her. She had invited him in and gone to call James. Davies said he needed to talk to James concerning a problem at the lab, but Amy could see right through that pathetic little story. She had left him in the kitchen, and when she came back he was gazing out of the window, admiring the view across the open fields.

'Doctor Davies, I have something for you,' she had said.

He turned to face her, and as he did she thrust the hunting knife deep into his heart. The surprise on his face was fascinating to watch; his eyes bulged, his mouth opening and closing like a fish out of water. His hands went to the handle of the knife and grasped at it; he didn't have the strength to pull it out, and all he could do was stare at her as his life ebbed away. His heart finally stopped beating, his brain closing down as he slumped to the floor. One more busybody who had learned the hard way not to interfere in her quest.

She had decapitated him and dumped his body in the bath; she placed the head in a cardboard box and drove into town, where she addressed the box and put it into an express delivery for Mitchell. She chuckled at the thought of Mitchell opening the box, and the shock she would receive. These people would never learn; they just weren't smart enough to outwit her.

She drove to Davies's house in his own car, and let herself in with his door key. She had gone through his files until she found the one she needed. Marked James Elliot, it contained all the notes from James's therapy sessions and confirmed her suspicions that Davies suspected her. She then drove to the research centre, where she gave Barton the security guard a winning smile.

'You know I shouldn't let you in without a pass, Mrs Elliot; but seeing that it's you, we'll let it go this time.'

She gave him a dazzling smile as she passed through the barrier; the fool hadn't even bothered to check whether James was in work. She had no problem in gaining access to his office; the secretary was not at her desk, so she walked straight in. She quickly rifled through the filing cabinets and found a duplicate copy of James's file. She placed it inside her coat and was out of the building within minutes; she waved at Barton on her way out of the gates, giving him another smile. Men were so easily pleased; she turned into the traffic flow and headed for home, her task completed. She was safe again now; as long as Davies hadn't talked to Collins, she would be fine. She would deal with that problem if and when it arose.

Chapter Thirty Seven

Collins had undergone a gruelling interrogation by her senior officers. They were demanding a result, just as she had expected, and the case had now taken on a new dimension of importance because the latest victim was in the public eye. A well known figure, they had told her:

'We can't have this person running around killing important people. It's just not on; if you can't come up with a result we will have to bring in somebody who can.'

Collins was furious. It made no difference that Davies was well known; all the victims were the same to her. Davies was slightly more personal because she had known and worked with him, not because he was a celebrity. She had to bite her tongue. She felt that they were getting closer to Amy; she was changing her pattern, and that would cause her to make mistakes. She didn't want the case handed over to someone else, not at this point; so she promised her superiors that she would obtain a result within five days. She knew this was a little reckless, but she was desperate. She had to flush Amy out, pressurise her into making a major mistake.

She would start by searching Davies's property. She knew that he often worked from home, and somewhere in his files could well be the name of the suspect. Davies had not been killed for fun, she was sure; Amy had only killed girls up to now. She must have known that Davies suspected her, and decided to kill him to protect herself. The indications were that the killer might be someone that Davies worked with or at least had regular contact with. It was a massive coincidence, but she was now convinced that the place to look was at those close to Davies. It was a possibility that Davies had actually discussed the case with the killer, or perhaps more likely that the killer knew about the case through a third party. Collins wondered if Amy had been able to keep one step ahead of the task force because she had inside information; she had been very careful not to leave any evidence which could be used positively against her. There was never any blood or other bodily traces on or around the victims. How much did Amy know, wondered Collins.

She arrived at Davies's property to conduct the search herself; she set the forensic team to searching all the other rooms with a fine tooth comb. She was sure that the answer would lie in the study, somewhere amongst the mountain of papers and files she was now confronted with. Two detectives were with her to help with the search. She briefed them on what she was looking for and left them to trawl through the stacks of files, while she lit up the computer which was sat on the desk that Davies used in the centre of his study.

Collins and her team were there for hours; at the end of the search they had turned up nothing. If there were any records on the computer they had been erased. There wasn't a single file which could be connected to the killings. She made a note to have the computer taken to the police IT department. She knew that any deleted files could be recorded on the hard disk; it wasn't that easy to delete material from a computer permanently.

She looked around the room. Had the killer been here? Had she erased the files? It was possible. Collins checked all the notepads and found some pages had been removed. She held the page underneath the light; she could see indentations in the paper, but couldn't make out any words. She placed all the notepads into evidence bags for examination back at the labs.

If there was anything on them, the technicians would find it. They were wizards at that sort of thing; their lab was equipped with the best equipment money could buy and their expertise was second to none. It was time to leave the house and go over to the research centre where Davies had worked. She left the forensic team to their painstaking task and took the rest of her team to carry out interviews with all the staff at the centre. The mood was sombre when they reached the centre; news had spread around the premises of the Doctor's death, and people were in varying states of shock and disbelief. Some of them had worked with Davies for years and were clearly distraught at the news; others were more composed. The Research Director met Collins and her team in the reception area, and promised full cooperation with the inquiry to find Davies's killer. He organised the personnel officer to send the staff in three at a time to be interviewed; he had set aside three offices for Collins and her colleagues.

The one person Collins had wanted to interview was the secretary; she was closest to Davies and would be privy to his most confidential information. It wasn't unknown for doctors to discuss their cases with trusted employees like a secretary; he may have given her information that would be vital in finding the killer. Unfortunately, upon hearing the news of the death, the secretary had collapsed in a state of shock and had been taken to hospital. She was under sedation and wouldn't be fit to interview until the morning, the consultant had told her colleagues. Collins felt frustrated; every time she thought she had some small opening, the door slammed in her face. Her last hope for today would be to look at Davies's files. She requested that she be shown to his office but was left waiting for a full ten minutes before the facility's Director appeared.

'I think we have a problem here, Detective Collins; the files you are asking to see are highly confidential. The Doctor could never reveal their contents; it would breach his oath. In exceptional circumstances you could ask for a court order to see them, but it would be very difficult due to the Data Protection Act.'

Collins stared at the Director hard and took a deep breath; she would have gladly throttled him right at that moment. How could he be so damned clinical about this? He himself had known Davies for a good many years, and yet he talked about him as though he didn't even know him.

She chose her words carefully. She had to keep her cool; technically the Director was right, but if these were not exceptional circumstances then what were?

'I can see your problem Director, but I really think that Doctor Davies's oath died with him. I understand the records are in your care, but we are trying to catch a mass murderer and I need all the cooperation I can get.'

'If you do find anything in his files it won't stand up in a court of law, Detective; you know that, don't you?'

'Yes, I know that; I'm looking for information that may give us the killer's name. If we find the killer we will have all the evidence we need. I need to look at those files and I need to look now. Any delay could cost another innocent girl her life.'

The Director had wavered, but now he agreed to show Collins to the files she needed. He opened the door to Davies's office with a master key and let Collins enter. He didn't leave; instead, he sat on the leather chesterfield in the corner of the room and watched Collins like a hawk as she searched, first the filing cabinets and then the stacks of loose files from the shelves. She found nothing; she checked the desktop notepad and the diary, and once again pages appeared to have been removed. She placed both objects in evidence bags and informed the director that the forensic team would be here shortly to carry out a detailed search of the office.

The Director agreed to stay late and assist the team personally; he felt it was his responsibility, he told Collins. She agreed and thanked him for his cooperation; she went back to the office downstairs and asked for another employee to be sent in for interrogation.

The employees all seemed eager to help; they just didn't know anything. It was so frustrating. Davies had been a very private person and didn't get involved with his colleagues on a social level; he only had one or two friends outside of work, and they were being interviewed right at this moment. They finished the interviews by seven o'clock and decided enough was enough for one day; it had been a long and harrowing day for all of them.

They had all known Davies, and had taken it personally when he had been killed; she wanted her team fresh for the following day. There were two employees off work sick today, she discovered; she would come back tomorrow to interview those two personally. She wasn't very hopeful, but it was worth a long shot; one of them had been seeing Davies for consultations over his marriage problems, she was told. There were no records, but Davies would probably have treated it as a favour to a fellow employee, or so the Director had said. Collins and her team left the premises and headed for their respective homes; they all needed the rest. Each of them would relax in their own way this evening, all of them knowing that tomorrow was going to be another long, long day.

Chapter Thirty Eight

Collins was hard at work in the Task Force incident room. Her whole team had been in that morning, and they had carried out a review of the case. They had only included the most recent murders; all those within the last twelve months had been included. Collins considered that there was too much information to look at if they reviewed them all; they could get a shorter but just as accurate picture by using the more recent murders. The lab was still working on the notepads she had retrieved from both the research centre and Davies's home; the search of the registry records had revealed that none of the women they had checked were the one they sought. It was a possibility that Amy was a second name.

Collins was further becoming convinced that Amy was an exceptionally clever adversary. She had stayed one step ahead of the chase all the way through the investigation, and Collins was now convinced that she had received inside information. Someone had tipped her off; maybe inadvertently, but still they had tipped her off. She had made a mistake in killing Davies; she had revealed that Davies was on to her, which must mean that there was evidence to be found there.

Collins had decided to go back to the research centre today to interview the secretary, and the two employees who had been off sick yesterday. The answer must lie there somewhere. All the pieces were there, Collins could feel it; the luck was turning their way. She was feeling positive now, more so than she had done for months. It was tinged with sadness as she thought of Davies; she had lost a fine colleague, but that only made her more determined that his death wouldn't be in vain. She was going to nail this killer and soon, she told herself.

Collins was interrupted by a junior detective.

'This just arrived in the morning post, boss; for your eyes only.'

She took the letter from him; it had been posted the previous day and showed a Manchester post mark. She opened it carefully with a letter knife and spread the folded sheet on her desk. It was another picture; this time it showed two headless chickens instead of one. In the bottom corner was written 'From Amy Jayne', and at the top was a smiley face. Collins stared at the picture; the audacity of the bitch! She really was taunting them, just as Davies had told her she might. Why was it different though? This time there were two chickens; did that mean anything, or was it just Amy's sick sense of humour?

Amy was near; she could feel it. She was getting over-confident and that would finish her, Collins knew. She photocopied the picture and bagged it for the lab; she doubted that there would be anything on it, but it still had to be checked. She pinned the copy to the wall so that all of her team could see it. They would be even more determined when they saw the taunting headless chickens; they would take it as a personal insult. One of her officers was staring at the picture; he was deep in thought.

'Boss, you got the last picture, with one chicken, just before Davies was killed,' he said.

'That's right, Dave; go on.'

'Well, what if she's planning to kill another chicken? Another headless chicken, another one of our team?'

Collins stared at him and then at the picture.

'If the headless chicken is supposed to represent Davies' death, then it would be reasonable to assume she is going to kill another team member, or is at least planning to,' finished Dave.

Collins blinked hard at the picture; she hadn't seen it. She had thought it was just gloating on Amy's behalf; what if Dave was right? But the team had all been in the office that morning ... all apart from Mitchell.

'Dave, get onto Mitchell's surveillance team, I want a check on her right now,' barked Collins, urgency in her voice. It took a millisecond for Dave to understand what Collins was suggesting. Mitchell had become part of their team, but she was the only one who hadn't been in the incident room that morning. He picked the phone up and spoke to control.

'I need to speak to SB 1, urgently,' he emphasised to the operator. SB1 quickly came on the line.

'Hello, Dave; what's the problem?' he asked.

'I need you to check on your subject right now; we need a visual, ASAP.'

'We're right on it,' said the detective as he left the passenger seat of the unmarked police vehicle that was sat opposite Mitchell's apartment block.

His colleague had sounded worried; he wondered what all the fuss was about. He knocked anyway, but there was no answer; he tried the phone, still no answer. He called back to the office.

'Dave, we can't get an answer here, I don't think she's in.'

'Well have you seen her go out?' he demanded.

'No, we assumed she was here when we swapped with the night shift. We didn't ask. Sorry, Dave; what do you want us to do?'

'Hold the line while I speak to the boss.'

Dave explained to Collins that Mitchell wasn't answering the door. Collins had already tried her land line and mobile phones, and had got no answer. Something was wrong here, she could feel it; her stomach was knotting up.

'Kick the door in, now!' she told Dave.

He related the message down the phone to the waiting detective, who immediately went offline to carry out his orders. Collins picked up the phone and dialled the home number for one of her night shift team; he came on the line still half asleep and angry at being woken, but his mood changed when he realised it was Collins.

'Sorry boss, I haven't had much sleep,' he said.

'Never mind that, Colin; did you log Mitchell in or out last night?'

'We didn't see her, boss; I thought she was home when we started our shift. I didn't actually ask the day shift.'

The line went dead; Collins was on the phone to yesterday's team leader asking the same question.

'Sorry, boss,' was the reply, 'we heard about the incident with Davies's head, and that Mitchell was in a bad state of shock; we assumed she had gone to hospital or stayed somewhere else for the night. She certainly didn't come back before we went off duty; have you asked the night shift?

There was no answer. Collins was on her feet, heading for the lift, shouting orders to her team members; she wanted everyone out on the street. How the hell had this happened, she asked herself; this was a monumental cock-up. Her team should have known exactly where Mitchell was; they had taken their eyes off the ball. Collins was hoping that Mitchell had stayed with friends or colleagues. The team leader at Mitchell's apartment called Collins as she drove to the newspapers premises; they had forced an entry, and there was no sign of Mitchell. She cursed as she ended the call; this was turning into a disaster. She arrived at the newspaper offices and went straight to the editor's office.

'Donald, I need you to tell me that Kate Mitchell stayed with one of her colleagues last night,' she said without ceremony.

The editor blinked; he could see that Collins was extremely agitated. After the events of yesterday everyone was on edge; he felt a cold ball in the pit of his stomach.

'I'm sorry Detective Collins, but I thought Kate had gone home. I didn't see her after she went to the rest room with the doctor; I assumed that one of your people had taken her home.'

There was panic in his voice; Collins could see he was genuinely worried.

'I'm afraid we don't know where she is, Donald; everybody has been assuming one thing or another and it's caused a real mix up, I need to speak to everyone who was in the office when Kate opened the parcel; can you do that for me, Donald?'

The editor picked up his phone and spoke to his assistant.

'On the double Andrew, it's very important,' he told him.

All of the staff was assembled within five minutes; Collins didn't want to waste time so she addressed them as a group.

'I'm Detective Collins, I'm in charge of the Head Hunter inquiry,' she told them; she didn't like using that phrase, but it was the most effective way of getting their attention.

'You are all aware of yesterday's events; I need to know if Kate Mitchell stayed at any of your homes last night, and if not do any of you know where she might have stayed? Has she got family or friends in the area?'

They were all staring at Collins, not quite understanding the implications of what she was asking; one by one they shook their heads, and Collins felt her heart sink.

'Okay, Kate is missing; this is very important. I need to know who saw her last, at what time; who was she with and where did she go?'

The editor spoke first, 'She left the room with the doctor, and I assume that they went to our staff rest room. We have a room set aside for anyone who isn't feeling well, a kind of sick bay if you like.'

'Did anyone see her after that?' asked Collins.

There was no reply to her question; just a shake of heads and concerned looks.

'Have you got the number for the doctor, Donald? We need to speak to him straight away.'

'I haven't got the number; it wasn't me who called her.'

'Her? It was a woman? Which one of you called her?' she looked around the confused faces.

'Did any of you here call the doctor for Kate?'

More shaking heads; she felt the cold grip of fear creeping steadily upwards towards her chest; she felt like she was being squeezed by a giant hand. She had to stay calm; panic wasn't going to help the situation.

'Who spoke to the doctor and what did she say?' Collins asked.

'I did,' said Andrew, the assistant editor.

'I saw her come in the room and asked how I could help her; she said she had been called to attend to a patient in a state of shock. She gave Kate's name.'

'Then what did she do?' asked Collins.

'Asked for somewhere private to treat Kate; she said she would probably need to sedate her and it would be better if she had somewhere to lie down. I showed her to the rest room,' finished Andrew.

'Didn't you think to ask for ID?' asked Collins angrily.

'I'm sorry Detective, but I assumed that one of my colleagues had called her. Anyway, when was the last time you asked a doctor for ID?'

He was right, of course; she wouldn't have asked for ID either. He was also another one who had assumed; she was becoming sick of hearing that word. Everyone knew you shouldn't assume anything, but they were all guilty of doing it at sometime; it was just a human weakness.

Collins listened as the few staff who had seen the 'doctor', described her. They all agreed in their descriptions; mid-twenties, medium-length dark hair; she was petite and well dressed. She had worn tinted glasses so nobody could give her eye colour. Collins thanked the staff and went to the editor's office; he had given her the use of all his facilities while she was in the building. She made frantic calls to Task Force HQ and put out a general alert for both Mitchell and Amy. She asked for, and got, extra resources from her Chief Constable; he wouldn't want a dead journalist on his hands, she knew.

She now had hundreds of officers, all over the immediately surrounding area, working on her behalf; knocking on doors in the area, looking at CCTV footage from local shops and businesses. The forensic team were combing the rest room, which was the last known whereabouts of Mitchell, for the slightest clue; but Collins didn't expect anything to turn up in that direction. Amy was far too clever for that. She had walked right into the lion's den and abducted Mitchell from under their noses; she may even have still been in the building when Collins herself was there. Collins cursed her again; yes, she was clever, but Davies had said that her conceit might well be her undoing. She hoped so. If Kate Mitchell was killed she would blame herself; she had failed in her duty in the worst way, and she had underestimated Amy. Her career would be over and she would be looking for new employment, not a prospect she relished at this time of her life.

She needed to get away from town; it was choking her, being in the midst of this chaos. Everyone was rushing round, shouting and swearing. She had half the force looking for Mitchell; she would take her own car and drive out into the countryside where she could breathe and collect her thoughts. If anything came up, her team could contact her by mobile phone. It wasn't really the right thing to do at a time like this, but she felt it would help her think if she could just sit for a short time in the open air, without anybody to disturb her for a while.

She left the busy city and joined the A34 going towards the Cheshire border. It was only a few miles to drive, but it left you in a different world, one of relative tranquillity. She would recharge her batteries for a few hours and come back refreshed, ready for whatever the rest of the day might bring.

Chapter Thirty Nine

As Collins and her team had slept the previous night, Amy had been busy. She was on her way to the farm; she had her latest piece in the car boot, and mother was going to be so pleased. It was still breathing. She had administered enough sedative to keep it unconscious for twelve hours, and when it had begun to stir she had simply given the piece another small dose. She arrived at the farm and removed her piece from the car boot; she dragged it across the yard, through the dried mud and dust, and into the barn. She opened the trapdoor and threw it down the dark hole; she heard it land with a dull thud and a crack. It sounded like it may have been a broken bone, but that really was of no consequence now. It wouldn't be needing bones where it was going.

Amy climbed carefully down the steps to the cellar floor; she checked that the piece was still unconscious and then dragged it over to the centre of the room. She had fixed two large hooks into the ceiling beams and attached a rope to each one; she hoisted her piece up and tied the ropes around each wrist so that it was standing. Its feet were barely touching the floor, and its arms were raised and spread in the crucifix pose.

Amy carefully cut away the upper clothing; she cut a strip off the shirt to make a gag which she fastened in place so that it cut into the piece's mouth. She took a step backwards and admired her piece; it must be in its late thirties, but the body was still in magnificent shape thought Amy as she ran a critical eye over it. Men would love a body like that, she thought; what a pity none would ever see it again in its present form. She laughed at the ease with which she had obtained the piece; she had taken a massive gamble in collecting it. She would never have believed they could be so incompetent.

It was almost time to start. Amy felt the excitement rising throughout her body, the tingling, ecstatic feeling starting from her toes and spreading upwards to pervade every part of her body. She reached into her pocket and took out the smelling salts; she placed them under the piece's nose, and almost instantly it came awake. The eyes were adjusting to the light, straining to take in its surroundings; Amy could see that Kate Mitchell was tough. She wasn't panicking, and she was trying to evaluate her position and her surroundings.

Mitchell's eyes were becoming adjusted now; she could see the heads, sat on their shelves around the walls, and she could see the large urn in the centre with the evil-looking eyes gazing out over the room. Her own gaze settled on Amy; she studied her with professional interest. Even though she was tied and knew that she was unlikely to escape this place, unless by some miracle Collins had discovered she was missing, she was still detached enough to be interested in Amy. She was looking for some outward sign of madness, some sort of deformity; she didn't know what she was looking for, but it wasn't there. Amy appeared normal until she started speaking. She was laughing softly to herself, a childlike laugh; then her voice changed, a deeper, harsher laugh, and she was staring at Mitchell, her eyes like saucers, her face covered in a broad, manic grin.

Mitchell watched Amy pick up a knife and cleaver from the holdall at her side; she was talking to someone, and Mitchell strained to hear. Mother; she was talking to her mother. What had Davies said about that? She couldn't remember; the pain from her arm was becoming intense as it swelled around where it had been broken. She didn't remember breaking it but she knew it was broken. Another voice boomed out.

'Now, you worthless little bitch! Do it now!'

Mitchell was startled; she couldn't tell where that voice had come from but it was close to Amy. There was loud laughter; the same voice again, cruel and mocking. Mitchell was chilled to the bone; that voice was pure evil. She could see Amy laughing as well, but the other voice was so loud that she couldn't even hear Amy's voice over it.

Mitchell's senses had become alert now that the adrenalin was kicking in; she flicked her eyes around the room as far as she could, taking in the dozens of heads on the shelves around the walls. She could smell damp; it must be a basement or cellar, she thought. The single electric light cast strange dancing shadows along the walls as it swayed slightly from the breeze she could feel at her back. Directly ahead was the urn; the eyes were piercing and evil. She wondered what they meant. Her eyes went back to Amy; she was trembling, and laughing, her laughter rising in pitch to be almost hysterical. The other voice boomed again.

'Do it now, I want the heart!'

Amy walked towards Mitchell, her knife held out in front of her. Mitchell was staring at the knife, intrigued. This was the weapon that had killed so many people; Amy raised the knife to strike. The grin was fixed on Amy's face as she delivered a massive blow to Mitchell's chest; the knife cut cleanly through bone and sinew, piercing Mitchell's heart. She was lucky; the knife severed the main arteries to her heart. She lost consciousness and was dead before she had her head hacked from her body.

Amy ripped the knife through Mitchell's flesh; she opened the chest and ripped out the heart. She was out of control now, ripping at the heart with her teeth, swallowing the pieces before she had chewed them properly. With her other hand she hacked at Mitchell's head; it made a bloody mess but finally the head slid off the body, hanging on by a single piece of sinew. Amy hacked through it, cutting into the thigh as the sinew snapped and the head dropped, face first into the dust on the floor. She picked up the head by the hair, staring into the lifeless eyes; then she walked over to where Mother waited, and held it up for her to approve. She was sure she saw Mother's eyes smile; just a flicker, and then it was gone. She was elated; Mother was pleased with her. She lifted the piece and placed it next to Mother on the shelf. Amy stood back and admired the piece; it really was quite striking, she thought. A perfect piece to sit at Mother's right side. She looked at the time; it was getting late, so she would have to dispose of the waste tomorrow night. Amy would bring the chain saw to chop it up. It would be nice a treat for the foxes.

Amy threw off her clothes when she reached the house and ran them through a quick wash cycle; by the time she had showered and had a bite to eat, the clothes were washed and dried and ready to wear again. She packed up her tools in her holdall and locked up the farmhouse. She had to hurry home; she knew James would be awake for work in a couple of hours. She would have time to finish her waste disposal tomorrow night, or tonight she corrected herself. My, doesn't time fly she thought, as she left the dirt track and joined the main carriageway of the bypass.

She thought briefly of Collins and her team of headless chickens; in a few hours they would be running around frantically, searching for their pet journalist. She would let them search; it would keep the fools busy for a while. Amy whistled, and hummed her favourite tune as she drove. Things were going so well for her; she couldn't remember being so happy in a long time.

Chapter Forty

Collins had driven to a beauty spot in north Cheshire. As she sat on the edge of the rock she could see for miles over the Cheshire plains. Her mind was on Kate Mitchell; she prayed that they could find her in time. She couldn't bear to think of her friend going through the ordeal that the other victims had suffered, but she had to prepare herself for the worst scenario.

She looked across to her left and could see the city of Manchester, spreading out in a sprawling mass of factories and housing projects. A dirty cloud of smog hung over the city in the clear blue sky; she would soon have to make her way back into the urban jungle, with its filthy streets and run-down estates. The shiny glass and steel buildings of the inner city regeneration schemes stood above all the squalor. While they built and admired their shiny palaces, the people were still living in the same misery, in the same deprivation that they had always known. Palaces were no use to them, but they must be some use to somebody; they kept building them.

She shook her head; she could see the clinical research centre about three miles distant to the south. She walked back to her car, started the engine, and rejoined the A34 driving towards the research centre. She would finish doing the interviews; she still had two staff members to see as well as the secretary.

Davies's secretary was still visibly shaken; she had been with him for many years, but she was a professional and she would carry out her duties to the best of her ability, regardless of the circumstances. Collins asked her about Davies and his work.

'Did the Doctor have anyone here that he was counselling, Sarah?' she asked.

'Only James; James Elliot, from the Pharmaceuticals Division. He was having sleep problems; the doctor was giving him some informal advice. He was very good like that,' she sniffed.

'This James,' Collins enquired, 'he works in the building?'

'Yes, he works on the next floor; he's a pharmacist, and he's a very pleasant young man.'

'Is he married?'

'I don't think so, but I think he has a partner. I don't know him socially.'

'Can you show me his personnel file?' asked Collins.

Sarah went to the filing cabinet in the corner and produced a thick file which she handed to Collins. Collins opened the file and read through it. Elliot sounded like a model employee; he had a good education and employment history, and worked on producing new drugs to combat various clinical ailments. Access to drugs, Collins noted; but there was nothing else out of the ordinary. The form for next of kin on his job application was blank; he had no surviving family, it said.

'Do you have a name and number for his partner, Sarah?'

'If I have one it will be in my desk diary.'

She found the details in her diary and wrote the name and number down on a piece of paper which she handed to Collins. It was a mobile number, but what made Collins's heart leap into her mouth was the name, 'Amy', printed in neat block capitals underneath the number. The adrenalin kicked in immediately; Collins was on her feet.

'Can you have James Elliot brought down here right away Sarah, please?'

Sarah wasn't facing Collins; she was looking out in to the car park.

'I'm afraid you're too late, Detective; he's just leaving. That's him driving through the gate.'

Collins spun round; she could see a dark green, five-door saloon car driving slowly through the gate. She snatched the file containing Elliot's address from the table and ran from the office, leaving the secretary open-mouthed in astonishment.

She raced to her own car, and had her engine started and the car moving in record time. She could see the green saloon heading down the B road towards the A34 as she left the car park with a screech of tyres, the stone chips peppering an indignant security guard on the legs.

She followed Elliot at a safe distance; she would follow him home and see if she could spot Amy. She would decide how to handle it then; she didn't have her radio with her, but she could use her mobile to call for back up if she needed to.

They weren't driving long before Elliot turned off the main road onto a side road which ran through a small, well-to-do housing estate; the saloon pulled in at the end house and James Elliot got out of the vehicle. He walked to the front door and let himself in to the house; Collins was sure he had looked back and seen her, but she decided to wait a few minutes and try to catch sight of Amy.

Not more than two or three minutes had passed when the door opened and a young woman with dark, wavy hair and tinted glasses left the house. She got into the green saloon car and drove off down the road, passing Collins who had slumped down in her front seat in the hope that Amy wouldn't spot her. Collins's heart was racing; all that time searching for Amy and she had been practically on their doorstep. She wasn't going to escape now, thought Collins. She stayed at a safe distance behind her quarry as they drove back down the A34 towards Congleton.

Amy indicated and turned off the main road. There was what appeared to be a dirt track leading through the trees; Collins parked her car at the side of the road, taking her mobile phone and her telescopic baton just in case she ran into trouble. She made her way down the lane, keeping to the cover of the trees, until she saw Amy's car parked at a gate; the door was open, but there was no sign of Amy. Collins heard a door slam; Amy re-emerged from the gate and got into her car. Collins slid down a bank out of sight as Amy drove back out onto the main carriageway. She could either follow Amy or search the premises she had just visited in the hope that she would find Mitchell. Collins decided to search for Mitchell; she remembered Davies saying that the killer would have a lair. Maybe this was where the lair was, and she was still hoping to find Kate alive.

Collins ran quickly to the farmhouse; she smashed a small window in the back door, entered the house, and carried out a systematic search. She started in the loft and then made her way down to the ground floor; it was all clear. There was nothing in the house; she had checked for false walls and a cellar, but there were no concealed entrances to be found.

She went quickly to the barn; she felt that time was short. If Mitchell was still alive she had to find her soon; this killer didn't usually keep her victims alive for long. Collins hoped that Amy would view Mitchell differently. She was a member of the team and Amy had communicated with her; it was a slim chance but Amy might just want to gloat at Kate before she killed her.

Collins searched the upper floor of the barn without success, and was just about to leave the building when she felt a hollow thud under her feet. The ground here was different, she saw; she scraped at the straw and earth and revealed a wooden board, which looked suspiciously like a door. She looked round the barn and found a stiff yard brush which she used to brush away the remaining dirt from the door. She could see a ring set into one end of the door, and leaned down to grip it with both hands. She pulled and, after a couple of tugs, the door lifted, revealing a set of steps leading down to what must be a cellar of some sort.

Collins went back to the barn door and listened for the sound of a vehicle; she didn't think that Amy had seen her. She must have forgotten something and returned to retrieve it. She would take a chance that Amy would be back home by now; she would phone in to the incident room if she found anything in the cellar. The team could be out here in force within half an hour, and if she needed back-up she could use local Bobbies.

Collins stepped backwards, putting her left foot on the first rung of the ladder; it was strong enough to hold her weight, but she climbed down the rest of the ladder carefully, in case it was rotten. She soon found herself on solid ground again. The room was dark; she couldn't see more than a couple of feet in any direction. She moved slowly away from the trapdoor; something touched her face as she moved forward, and then brushed it again. She reached up and felt a thin cord dangling from the ceiling; she pulled, and for a few seconds was blinded by the flood of light. She was looking directly at the bulb when the light went on, and had to wait until her eyes cleared and adjusted.

She walked slowly forward. She could see a body hanging from the ceiling by its arms; the head was missing, the arms raised upwards and outwards in that crucifix pose that she had seen only days before. She knew it was Kate Mitchell even before she reached the body, not because she knew Kate Mitchell's body but because there, right in front of her, was Kate Mitchell's head. It sat on a shelf slightly askew where the neck had been hacked to pieces. Collins let out a tortured wail; she was too late to save her friend. She had made too many mistakes, and now Kate was dead. She sobbed as she looked at the other victims; there were dozens of heads all around the room, and she recognised some from photographs in the files.

She got out her mobile phone and speed dialled Task Force HQ, but there was no signal because she was underground. She decided it would wait a few minutes. She had to keep her cool and be professional; the killer was still out there, and she had to make sure that her reign of terror was brought to an end. She looked at Kate's body, hanging like a butchered carcass; she had been ripped to pieces. Collins felt the fear turning to anger; she cursed to herself out loud as she stepped closer to Kate's head. Next to it was a large clay urn, and on the urn she could see a pair of evil-looking eyes had been painted. She stared back at the eyes; it was a strange feeling but they felt almost hypnotic. She couldn't seem to drag her gaze away; it was as if she was locked in a trance.

A massive crash behind her shocked her out of her wits; she knew it was the trap door closing. She turned slowly, deliberately, not making any quick movements. She was looking into the light; a figure was standing at the bottom of the ladder. Amy stepped forward; she had on a black dress, a special-occasion type dress. Collins wondered if the special occasion was their meeting; she slid her telescopic baton into her hand, careful not to let Amy see it.

'Hello, Amy. We meet at last,' said Collins, more casually than she felt. She was pressing her speed dial button on her mobile phone, but wasn't hopeful it would work. Amy smiled.

'Hello, Detective Collins. I don't recall inviting you to my house.'

It was the way she spoke that chilled Collins's blood; so matter-of-fact, as though they were discussing the weather or some other trivial matter. She was feeling fear like she had never known before; Amy was totally in control and she knew it. Collins knew it too; if she was going to get out of this place alive she was going to have to overpower Amy and disable her. Collins could feel her hands trembling; sweat was running down her back and she could feel the cold grip of her fear taking a hold of her senses. She felt unable to move.

'We can talk about this, Amy; if you give yourself up I'll see that you are treated fairly. We have people who can help with problems like yours.'

'And I don't recall telling you to use my Christian name. Mrs Elliott will do, thank you.'

'I'm sorry, I didn't realise you were married,' said Collins, trying to placate her.

'Oh, yes; me and my James will never be separated.'

She was smiling now; she looked almost pleasant until Collins looked into her eyes. They were bulging, the pupils dilated and fixed; they looked like white saucers in the dark shadows of her face. Collins slowly stepped towards Amy, letting the baton extend noiselessly. Amy didn't move, just stared, and smiled as Collins drew nearer.

'Mrs Elliot, will you give yourself up to me? We have doctors who can help with your problem,' Collins tried again.

'You don't seem to understand, Detective; I don't have a problem. Mother is happy and my quest is nearly over. You are the one with the problem.'

Collins rocked back as a loud voice boomed from Amy's mouth.

'Don't listen to the bitch, Amy! She's trying to trick you. She'll lock you up in a tiny cell, just like the cupboard!'

The voice changed again to a feminine whine.

'Not the cupboard!'

'Yes, the cupboard!' the booming voice returned. 'She'll lock you away in a little room, and you'll never, ever get out! You ate her bitch friend's heart, remember? You ate her heart! She will never forgive you for that!'

'I'm not listening to her, mother,' whimpered Amy.

Collins watched, fascinated at the different personalities having a conversation between themselves. She finally understood what madness meant now; she had to make an attempt to grab Amy and restrain her. Collins leaned forward on the balls of her feet, she was coiled like a spring; she leapt at Amy, swinging her baton as she did so, aiming for her head. She wanted to put her out of circulation; she was too dangerous to fight with, and she needed a knockout blow.

She watched as Amy, with the speed of a striking snake, ducked under her blow. Collins was caught off balance. Amy brought her hands up; one grabbed the inside of Collins's wrist, the other the back of her forearm. Collins felt her wrist snap as Amy used her own weight against her; she felt the pain shoot through her arm and fell forwards onto her face.

Through her pain Collins heard laughter; first, the shrill, high-pitched laughter of Amy, and then a deep, manic, blood-curdling peal of laughter that reverberated around the cellar. It seemed to tear at the air, bursting through Collins's eardrums with a deafening roar.

She felt hands grab her ankles and drag her away from the

trapdoor, to where that hideous urn sat on the shelf, watching over them like some vulture waiting for its prey to die. As they reached the urn Collins made a mighty effort; she rolled onto her back and jack-knifed her body; her feet shot out and caught Amy on the side of the face.

Amy staggered backwards into the shelves, catching the urn with her arm and sending it crashing to the floor, where it shattered into fragments and cloud of ash with a deafening crash.

Amy was momentarily stunned and Collins grasped the moment; she was on her feet and racing for the trapdoor. She reached the bottom rung and put her left foot on it; she heard a whirring, whistling noise as she raised herself to the second rung, and then felt a massive blow to the centre of her back. She crumpled in a heap at the bottom of the ladder; her arms and legs wouldn't move, but all of her senses were working. She saw Amy, her face already swelling where she had kicked her, coming towards her. Amy had a large hunting knife in her hand, and Collins could see it was already stained with blood; she watched Amy, unable to move any of her limbs.

She felt a tug at her back, and Amy stood over her with a fearsome-looking meat cleaver in her hand. It was dripping with blood; her own, she knew. Amy must have thrown it at her as she attempted to flee. It must have damaged her spine; it was over, she was going to die, and Amy was going to go on killing.

Amy dragged her, face down, across the rough floor, scraping skin from her cheeks; the voice boomed again

'Be careful with it's face, don't ruin it's face!'

Then Amy's voice again:

'Sorry, Mother; I won't ruin it, I promise you.'

Collins felt herself being turned over to lie on her back. She looked up into Amy's evil eyes; she felt only despair, and she hoped Amy would end it quickly. She had gambled and lost; now more innocent people would suffer because of her stupidity. She should never have come here alone, but it was too late for all that. Amy sat astride Collins's body; she had the knife in one hand and the cleaver in the other,

'You broke Mother's urn,' she said angrily, as she cut away the front of Collins's shirt.

Collins was beyond fear now; her professional mind had taken over, the one that had always striven to learn as much as she could take in; she was learning now, at first hand, how serial killers took their victims' lives.

Amy placed the point of the knife blade on Collins's chest and pushed down with both hands until it was buried to the hilt, never for a second taking her eyes off Collins; she wanted to see the fear in her eyes. She picked up the cleaver and started using it as a saw on Collins's neck, careful not to cut the main arteries; she wanted to take her head completely off without killing her. She wanted to hold it up and show Collins her own head in the mirror; she was laughing as she sawed, all the time staring into Collins's eyes. Amy didn't get her wish; Collins drew her last breath before Amy could finish the job.

Chapter Forty One

Amy was washed and dressed; she had finished Collins off quickly once she had died. It wasn't the same when they were dead; you couldn't watch their reactions. Collins had disappointed her; she thought she would have lasted a lot longer, but the blow to her back must have damaged her spinal cord. She cut the heart from the body and ate it while she sat astride it, hacking with her cleaver until the head was severed. She placed the head on the shelf next to Mothers' eyes; she had managed to save the eyes, at least. The rest of the urn was beyond repair. On the other side of Mother's eyes sat Mitchell; they were a fine pair of pieces to complete her collection. Her quest was over, and Mother had at last whispered the words she had longed to hear:

'Amy, I love you,' she had said.

Amy arranged all of her pieces neatly on the shelves and said goodbye to Mother before she left the cellar. There was no stinging rebuke, no scornful laugh or threats of the cupboard; just a tranquil silence.

Amy arrived home, exhausted. It had been a long and strenuous day. She was free of Mother now; Mother had gone, and she could live her life free from interference. She went upstairs to the bathroom and undressed; she threw the black dress to the floor along with her other clothes and her wig. She wouldn't be using them anymore. She smiled and hummed her favourite tune as the water from the shower jets massaged her tingling flesh, enjoying the freedom to be who she was at last.

James Elliott stepped from the shower; he was refreshed and felt like a new man. He went through to the bedroom, humming his favourite tune. He lay down on the bed; his mind was free of stress, his body completely relaxed. He closed his eyes and started to drift off to sleep.

'James.'

It was just a whisper. His eyes clicked wide open; it was Mother, and she had called him James. After all those years of being Amy, she had finally accepted him. His face lit up in a beaming smile.

'James,' she called again, this time louder and stronger.

'Yes, Mother?' replied James.

'I think it's time you got yourself a new wife. Amy is looking the worse for wear.'

James turned and looked at the mummified body of the girl called Amy. Yes, he thought; Mother was right. He rolled on to his side and pushed the body onto the floor. The bones clattered on the bedside cabinet and he dusted the duvet down where the body had left flakes of skin. He rolled over to his back again, a contented smile on his face.

'Yes, Mother; you're right,' he said lovingly.

He was excited now; he shut his eyes, and tried to sleep. He slowly drifted off, a smile still playing over his face in anticipation of the killing hour.

*

His eyes clicked wide open ...